STORMS
NEVER LAST

STORMS
NEVER LAST

ANNA'S TOWN BOOK III

ROBERT COLEMAN

STORMS NEVER LAST
ANNA'S TOWN BOOK III

iUniverse books may be ordered through booksellers or by contacting:

iUniverse
1663 Liberty Drive
Bloomington, IN 47403
www.iuniverse.com
844-349-9409

Because of the dynamic nature of the Internet, any web addresses or links contained in this book may have changed since publication and may no longer be valid. The views expressed in this work are solely those of the author and do not necessarily reflect the views of the publisher, and the publisher hereby disclaims any responsibility for them.

Any people depicted in stock imagery provided by Getty Images are models, and such images are being used for illustrative purposes only. Certain stock imagery © Getty Images.

ISBN: 978-1-6632-3859-7 (sc)
ISBN: 978-1-6632-3858-0 (e)

Library of Congress Control Number: 2022906820

Print information available on the last page.

iUniverse rev. date: 04/21/2022

Dedication

This book is dedicated to the memory of JT Coleman, who was my brother, my guardian, my mentor and my best friend. He gave me a home when I had none and treated me as if I were his own.

Prologue

A.C. Calloway moved his family from Big Flat Mississippi to Tupelo in the fall of 1951. He had suffered through three years of poor crops from flooding and had sold just about everything he owned to pay out of debt. He, his wife, Allie, and two sons, Willy and Zack, had moved into a small house on the grounds of the Purnell Lumber and Supply company. Pappy, as the boys called him, took a job managing the lumber yard for his old friend, Wayne Purnell. He and Wayne had served together in the Navy and were together when the Japanese bombed Pearl Harbor on December 7, 1941. Both were wounded and spent six months in a military hospital where their friendship was cemented forever. Both were decorated veterans.

The move to Tupelo got off to a rough start for his two sons when they had to confront the two meanest boys in Tupelo. It was at the Junior high school, where Zack met Annabelle Owens, one of the prettiest girls in school. In addition to being beautiful, she was also very smart and very brash. Their friendship quickly grew into something far more serious. The Calloway boys had become somewhat of heroes for teaching the McCullough's a lesson with a Louisville slugger bat. The McCullough's had been robbing students of their lunch money and striking fear into anyone who walked the streets around the school. The Calloway brothers had learned however, after their confrontation, that the McCullough's were desperate, and just trying to get enough money together to feed themselves and hire a doctor to see about their very sick mother. When Zack and Willy had learned why the boys were doing what they were doing, they wanted to help. When they went to Pappy to see if he could help Naught and Nate with their mother, a new friendship with the McCullough's began to develop.

Pappy had met Albert Davis, an old man who came to the lumber yard on a regular basis, and had befriended the old fellow who, was well into his eighties and in poor health. Albert had no family to take care of him and had no one to turn to when he fell ill. Momma and Pappy who had refused to let him go into a nursing facility, prepared a room for him and moved him into the house with the Calloway family. He soon became a part of the family and when the old man passed away, he left his entire estate to AC and Allie Calloway. The estate consisted of over a thousand acres of good farmland, and over a half million dollars in cash. There were also a hundred head of cattle as well. AC was now a very wealthy man, and when his friend Wayne, offered him a partnership in the business, AC accepted and the two men began an expansion of the business in Tupelo, and started two additional stores in West Point and Columbus. Tupelo was a thriving community, and they had also built a 36-unit apartment building on the west side of town.'

That Christmas Zack gave Anna a gold locket as their relationship grew more serious, then in the next year, Doctors at the center discovered that Anna had terminal cancer. When Anna learned that she was dying, she asked Zack to spend the night with her. That night they had their first sexual experience. Then, the Mysterious Doctor Luke appeared during the night and gave her medication. He also performed an ancient ritual on both Anna and Zack. The next morning when the Doctors checked on Anna, she had no sign of cancer. It had disappeared.

This presented problems for Anna and Zack, and for the hospital, for there was no Doctor Luke who worked at the hospital. Some legal proceeding followed, but with the help of Justin T. Webb, a local attorney, the problems were finally resolved, and Anna and Zack's bond grew stronger until Anna was killed in a terrible auto accident. [1]

A year had passed when AC and Allie took on two children to raise. Charlie and Robert Calloway were children of a distant cousin. Both the mother and father of the children had died of cancer and in their last will has asked AC and Allie to rear their children.

Charlie grew closer to Zack than she did the rest of the family. She also grew close to Annabelle and Anna's mother, When Anna was killed, she decided she did not want to be adopted by the Calloway family, but wanted to live with Anna's mother, Marie Owens.

The loss of Anna turned Zack's world upside down. His life changes when he assists the Webb law firm with a lawsuit filed by Anna's Mother Marie Owens.

1

Grief Takes Control

SORROW COVERED US LIKE of shroud of darkness, Charlie and me, as we left Columbus and Annabelle Owens, the love of my life, lying dead and buried behind the ivy-covered fences of Friendship cemetery. The clouds hung low and ominous over the small town, a light mist began to fall against the windshield of my old truck as I drove, lightening flashed far-off to the West and thunder rolled. The dreary weather just seemed to draw the two of us deeper and deeper into our despair.

Charlie had announced that she wanted to live with Marie Owens and be her daughter just before I dropped Marie off at her in-laws. This shocked and troubled me.

When I was just outside the city limits, I noticed that Marie had left her wallet on the dash of my truck. I saw a pay phone up ahead and pulled over. I called her father-in-law's number. Her Mother-in-law answered. I asked to speak to Marie. She came to the phone, and I explained to her why I called.

"Do you want me to bring the wallet to you?" I asked. "I am just barely out of town."

"Yes, if you don't mind, but since you are coming back, I have decided I want to go home. I will be waiting for you outside."

That answer took me by surprise and caused me to wonder if she had not left her wallet on purpose, for I knew her in-laws were expecting her to stay with them for a few days. The death of her only child and the real source for her reason for living was tearing her apart, and it showed in every fiber of her beautiful face. She seemed to be on an island of her own now, far away from family and friends. Her face showed that a storm was brewing inside. Her mind fixed only on one thing now: how to move forward without her daughter. However, grief comes in its own moment and stays until its own hour. Marie was just at the beginning of the storm, and I wanted to help her through the grieving period. I too was filled with sorrow, but I had a close family to lean on; Marie did not. She had lost both parents in a boating accident when she was a child, her husband in the war, and now the loss of her only daughter. She was a very broken and a lonely woman.

Minutes later I pulled into the drive. Marie and her in-laws stood huddled Just inside the garage, away from the cold drizzle. She turned and hugged them both, then opened the truck door and slid in beside Charlie. I didn't ask for an explanation for the change of heart. She would tell me when she was ready. I expected that Marie was being peppered with too many questions, and she just needed time to clear her mind and think things through. Sorrow, like joy always wanes with time. There would be little joy for Marie for her sorrow was too deep.

. Momma and Pappy both loved Charlie and Robert dearly and were hoping to adopt them soon. They would be devastated by the news that Charlie wanted to live with Marie Owens. Charlie lay her head across Marie's lap and Marie took my coat and covered her, for it was cool inside the truck and my heater did not work very well. There was little talk as we drove on into the darkness.

The rain finally ceased when we were a few miles out of Columbus, and I stopped in Aberdeen at Andy's Cafe and Texaco Station to use the restroom. Aberdeen was a beautiful old town, established in the 1830's, located on the banks of the Tombigbee River, with Magnolia lined streets, antebellum homes, columned mansion, and a few brick-covered sidewalks that had just about worn away, but tonight it was just a dreary old town, Charlie roused enough to ask me for a hamburger, but I reminded her that Momma was fixing supper for us and we would be home in less than an hour. I had heard her invite Marie to supper when we were leaving the cemetery, and she had declined the invite. Momma would be surprised that she had changed her mind, but I knew Momma would be happy that she came.

I bought Charlie a soda and chips to tide her over. I had forgotten that we had not eaten anything since morning. I bought coffee for Marie and myself. Charlie ate her chips and drank her bottle of Root Beer and then lay across Marie and slept again, with Marie running her hand through Charlie's long red hair. Marie cried again. I reached over and squeezed her arm and told her that everything would work out and she was going to be alright. I was not sure, however, that Marie would ever be alright again. She had seen too much sorrow in her life. She was a beautiful woman and only thirty-three years old. I hoped she would find someone to love her like I had loved Annabelle. She had love to give I knew, but I also knew it would have to be a special person. She took my hand and held it until Charlie stirred again. She would need me and Charlie for a while, and I wanted to be a good friend to her, for we had become much closer since Annabelle's death. Tragedy can push people apart or bring them closer. In our case it had cemented our relationship for the better.

I turned into our driveway a little before seven. The rain had stopped completely, but the clouds were heavy and there was no moon or stars to light the night sky. Charlie led the way up the front steps and opened the door. Squat came from his lair long enough to give us the sniff test but went back beneath the house when no one rubbed his head. Squat was getting older and did not have time for folks that paid him no attention. Squat was Pappy's dog for sure and he would go with Pappa to the farm every day. Momma said the dog had taken on Pappy's ways and was stubborn as a mule.

We walked into the house with the smell of fried chicken still in the air. Momma hugged Charlie and Marie, although she looked surprised to see Marie. Marie's eyes were still red from crying, and so were mine, which also brought tears to Momma's eyes.

Momma ushered all of us to the pine table in the middle of our dining room. Pappy was in his ladder-back rocking chair in the living room with Robert astraddle his knees. They were watching the Red Skelton Show on TV and Robert was laughing. Pappy got up and greeted Marie. Momma then asked us all to sit. Robert ran to the table.

Momma had fixed a plate of food for him, and he dove right into his food, not waiting for everyone to be seated. Robert had not gone to the funeral or the burial of Annabelle. Momma thought it might be too traumatic, so she had asked Joe Webb if he would take him fishing at the big pond on the farm. He was glad to do it and had picked the boy up an hour before we all left for the church in the morning. It had not occurred to me that no one had talked to him about Anna's death. I was surprised when he asked, "where's Anna?" He was looking to Pappy for an answer.

Pappy was taken off guard by Rob's question, but just kept eating and said, "Anna won't be coming –now eat your supper."

"Anna died didn't she Pappy?" Robert cried.

Pappy's eyes went first to Marie and then back to Robert. "Yes, she did Rob. She died trying to save a little boy about your age. She was a very brave Girl."

I don't know how Pappa knew what to say to Robert, but it seemed the right thing even though it upset the boy. Pappy always just seemed to know what was in a person's need to hear. How Robert had learned of Anna's death I did not know, and no one seemed compelled to ask.

Tears swelled in Robert's eyes, and he jumped from the table crying and ran to Momma. "I didn't want her to die, she was my friend," he sobbed, "I loved Anna."

Momma swept him into her arms and took him to the living room to her rocker. We could hear her talking in soft words to him. Soon we could hear only sniffles, and then there was only silence.

We finished our meal with very little talk. Everyone seemed to be lost in his own thoughts of the sad day. I was hungry and ate, but Marie Owens only picked at her food and drank her tea. Momma brought Robert back to the table so he could finish his meal. There was an awkwardness for a while, and then Marie thanked Momma for the meal but said she needed to go that she was very tired. She asked me if I would drop her off. She also apologized for dropping in on her for supper unexpectedly. I needed some time alone, to think, she said. Momma hugged her again and whispered something to her that I could not hear.

I went to my room and changed into Jeans and my Denim jacket. It was the one that Annabelle had told me she loved how it looked on me. She was with me the day I bought it. We had been window shopping on a Saturday afternoon.

Momma and Marie caressed at the door and then Marie hugged Charlie and we went to my truck. Minutes later I pulled into Marie's driveway and shut off the engine. She asked me if I would come in for a few minutes, that she had something she wanted to show me. I agreed, even though I was very tired. The rain had started falling again, we ran to her door. I sat on the couch in her living room while she went to the back of the house. A few minutes later she returned. She was wearing jeans and an Ole Miss Tee shirt. She was carrying three books. She handed them to me and said that she wanted me to have them. They were not books at all, but Annabelle's diaries.

"These are mostly about you, Marie said, from about the time you moved here from Big Flat."

I asked her if she would read some to me. Anna's and Marie's voices were so much alike that I had always had trouble knowing who was talking if they were in a room away from me. She said she would and decided to make some hot coco first. She made the coco and then came to the couch, bringing me a cup of the steaming brew. She sat beside me and drew her feet up beneath her and took the first diary and began to read.

November 27, 1951

Dear Diary:

We got two new students at our school today. Penelope and Jessica and I were sitting on the steps to Milam Jr. High when they crossed the street from Johnson's Grocery and service station. They were tall, thin, and straight with mops of dark hair. They took long strides as they walked the sidewalk by where we sat. I first thought they could have been twins, but as they came closer, I realized they were not. But no doubt they were brothers; one was a bit taller and heavier than the other, but both were very Handsome. Penelope had heard from Jessie that they were from a place called Big Flat. I did not know where Big Flat was, but the three of us agreed that we wanted to meet the new students. Neither of the boys were in my homeroom but the youngest was in Penelope's class. She had learned that his name was Zack Calloway, and that Big Flat was just a little town over past Pontotoc. At noon I saw him in the cafeteria and then later he was sitting alone on the steps. I decided we should introduce ourselves to Zack."

We pointed out the McCullough boys, who had the name of being the meanest boys in Tupelo. They were always hanging out down the street from Johnson's Grocery, on which the Calloway boys walked to school. He didn't seem to be concerned though. Me and penny decided that he might just be the best-looking boy in the whole school. I'm making it a point to get to know that boy better. My heart was beating faster, just thinking about him.

November 28, 1951

Dear Diary:

I got Mom to drop me off at school early today in hopes I would see the Calloway boy when he came across the street. I felt silly for chasing after a boy I hardly knew, but there was a feeling for him that I had never felt before. Penny and Jessie both rode the school bus to school, and I waited for them on the front steps to the building. We had just sat down when we saw the Callaway boys coming down the sidewalk approaching Johnson's Grocery. Both boys carried lunch sacks. Suddenly the McCullough boys broke out of the hedges, hitting the brothers from behind: knocking them to the concrete and jumping on top of them. The largest McCullough boy had the oldest brother pinned with his arms above his head. The youngest of the McCullough's had knocked Zack down and had him face down with his arms behind him.

The McCullough boys were yelling obscenities and threatening the new boys. The brothers could not move under the much heavier ruffians. I stood up and told Penny and Jessie I was going to help, but they held me and said that I would get in trouble if I left the school grounds and would be in trouble with my mother for sure.

There were dozens of students watching the attack, and not one person went to help the new students. I was so ashamed of our students for not going to their aid. Pretty soon the McCullough boys let the new students up and disappeared into the hedges with the lunch sacks of Zack and his brother in their hands. The Calloway's got up and dusted themselves off and crossed the road to the school. I made up my mind right then that if they were attacked again, I would go and try to help, even if I got in trouble for leaving school.

The boys did not sit down on the step but talked to each other away from the rest of the students.

Later in the day, I was sent outside to dust erasers, and I met Zack coming up the steps, I stopped and apologized for the school not coming to help when the McCullough boys attacked them. We all ought to be ashamed for the way we acted.

"It's our problem and we will have to deal with it," he stated. He said that he had not figured out just how they were going to deal with the problem, but they would.

You have some chalk, on your face he said reaching to brush it off. I moved my head at first but decided, quickly, that he was only trying to help. When he touched my face, I almost peed my pants. He gently wiped away the chalk. I felt weak in my knees when he smiled at me.

I told him thanks and left him standing there and went toward my classroom; when I looked back, he was still watching me and smiling.

I could think of nothing but Zack Calloway the rest of the day. I told Penny that I liked him a lot and meant for him to be my boyfriend. They teased me unmercifully the rest of the day, but I didn't care, for I liked that boy from Big Flat wherever that was.

As Marie continued to read, I finished my coco and leaned my head back against the sofa and listened to the sweet voice of Marie Owens Imagining it was Annabelle. In seconds I was asleep.

I awoke the next morning to the smell of bacon frying and coffee boiling on the stove. It was near seven O'clock. Marie had removed my shoes and covered me with a quilt.

"I'm sorry Marie. I was just so tired. Did you call my folks?"

"You don't need to apologize, Zack. And yes, I called your mother and told her that you were asleep and asked her if she wanted me to wake you and send you home. She told me to let you sleep. She didn't seem to be to happy about your staying overnight, but she said she knew you were very tired and needed rest."

Marie made me a plate of eggs and bacon and toast and set them on the table and motioned for me to sit. She made her a plate and set it down across from me. She brought us coffee and then she sat down. I asked to use the toilet.

"Down the hall on the right."

I had been coming to see Annabelle for the last five years but suddenly realized that I had never been past the living room in her house. After I used the toilet, I washed at the sink and then returned to the table. I was starved and ate everything she had put on my plate. There was not much conversation while we ate. When we had finished, eating. I told Marie that I needed to go home.

"I am not accustomed to staying out all night without telling my parents. Do you want me to help with the dishes?" I offered.

"No," she said, "you need to go."

I picked up Annabel's diaries and walked to the door. Marie followed me. We caressed and I held her for a moment. She smelled so much like Anna that I did not want to let her go, but finally we broke the hug. I started to step through the door but turned back. Tears were running down Marie's face.

"We need to talk with Charlie and my mother. Maybe we can do that this week."

She wiped the tears away shook her head. We were discussing Charlie, but no doubt her mind was on the loss of her daughter, Anna.

"Call me," she said. "We'll talk to Charlie and decide what to tell your mom."

"Are you going to be ok, Marie?" I asked. "If you want me to stay, I'll call and tell mom I'm going to stay with you a while longer."

"No," she said. "I do not think that would be a good idea. Call me tomorrow. I called my boss at the bank last night," and I told him I would like to take some time off. He told me to take the whole week if I wanted, more if I needed it. I just don't think I could concentrate on work right now"

"I think taking time off is a good idea. You need some time to sort things out, call if you need me."

I climbed into my truck and started for home and the tears came, streaming down my face. It seemed like a Tsunami of memories were flooding my brain. Everything that Anna and I had ever done together kept tugging at my heart. I finally pulled over to the curb rested my head on the steering wheel until the tears stopped coming. I dried my eyes the best I could for I did not want Charlie and Robert to know that I had been crying, and I was sure if they knew I was sad, they would cry too. When I had somewhat composed myself, I started for home again.

The rain had now slowed to a drizzle, and the kids came on the porch to meet me when I pulled into the drive. They wanted me to read to them. This is what we often did on Sunday afternoons when the weather was too bad to go outside. I went to the fold-out divan, in the living room, and the three of us, Charlie, Robert and I piled on. Charlie on one side and Robert Lewis on the other. I read to them from the *Adventures of Tom Sawyer*. It was a book that Robert had picked out at the city library more than a week before the death of Annabelle. Charlie and Momma had been reading it to Robert if I was not available. If I was there, However, they wanted me to read to them for I changed the sound of my voice to what I thought fit the characters in the story. They liked that. I read for a few minutes until the rain pounding on the tin roof of our house lulled the two children to sleep. Momma came and covered us with a blanket and soon I was in a deep sleep too, dreaming of Anabelle Owens. Momma called us to lunch just before noon, The rain had stopped, and the skies were clearing.

When We had eaten, we all went to the front porch and Pappy set up the folding table to play dominos with Momma sitting in the big rocker and helping Robert with his Counting. We played the rest of the afternoon away with everyone laughing and pointing fingers. My mind finally finding a few hours of respite from the thoughts of Annabelle Owens. The respite would be short-lived, however, for every fiber of my body ached for Anna. Even in my dreams she came to me, her tender smile lighting my world; the memory of her sweet voice stirring my senses.

2

Charlie Has A Plan

ON MONDAY, I WAS back in school, but my heart and mind were not really in it. My mind was foggy with only thoughts of Annabelle.' I was only taking two classes, for I had finished all my required courses at the end of the first term. I was out of class by ten in the morning, and I was given permission to leave campus and go to work at the Webb law firm. Mr. Webb let me work as much as I wanted and was letting me help him in court cases.

I was really getting the feel for what practicing Law was all about, and I was loving it. I would usually run errands, delivering mail and documents to the banks and other companies that the firm represented, I was also getting to know some of the most influential businessmen and women in Tupelo. I was using my truck for longer deliveries, so Mr. Webb would buy me a tank of gas each week and was paying me a straight twenty dollars a week. It was not much money, but I was happy with the arrangement.

The Law firm was closed on Wednesday afternoon, as were the courthouse and most businesses in the town. I would usually go to the farm and help Pappy with his chores. I was learning a lot about the farm business. Pappy and Joe Webb kept the place in top notch shape, so some days we would saddle the horses and ride over the entire farm checking on the cattle. Pappy also had hogs that he raised for our family and for Joe and would always furnish Mrs. McCullough a cured ham for her and Notch.

Mrs. McCullough was still living in the Davis house, even though she had received a bonus large enough to buy a house in the city when Pappy and Mr. Purnell sold the lumber company. She said she loved the farm and the solitude it provided for her, and she could have her own garden.

Pappy was happy that she wanted to stay, for she had planted flowers and shrubs, and she would call if there was any kind of problem with the animals. Notch kept the hogs and chickens fed. Pappy charged them no rent for living in the house. I figured there might be another reason too, on more than one occasion I had seen Mrs. McCullough and Joe Webb sitting in the front porch swing, having a glass of Iced tea. I thought to myself that they would make a fine pair. Joe was her closest neighbor. Pappy said that he was sure that Joe was looking out for her welfare; He said it with a sly grin and a wink.

Wednesday morning Charlie asked if we could go to the old church on Jefferson when school was out and talk awhile. She said she would meet me at Marie's. She and her friend Billy usually walked home together after school. She said Billy would be disappointed if she did not walk with him.

I drove to Marie's house just after four O'clock in the afternoon. Charlie and Marie were sitting in the porch swing eating popcorn. They had a quilt across their knees, and both were laughing. I parked the truck and walked up on the porch. Charlie moved over in the swing and motioned for me to sit. Marie asked if I wanted some popcorn. I said that I would eat some of Charlie's. I then reached over and took a huge hand full, leaving only a few kernels in her bowl. She was immediately off the swing spilling the rest of her popcorn and pulling the blanket off of Marie and also spilling Marie's bowl of popcorn. She was flailing her arms against my chest and calling me names.

"You are a gourd head," she yelled.

"And you are a bugle butt that's been kissing Billy Jackson."

"I ain't done no such thing. You take that back, she yelled! You are the Devil, Zack Calloway, and God's gonna get you for sure."

I grabbed her around the waist and put her across my knees and swatted her backside three times. I wrestled her down on the spread and was beside her holding her down and tickling her ribs. She was laughing and yelling for Marie to help.

"Get the hammer, Marie, or a butcher knife and bust this fool's noggin! I'm gonna pee if you don't let me up; I'm about to pop!"

Marie was down on the quilt with us and feinting trying to pull me off of Charlie. I pulled her down and they were both on top of me. Marie's pelvis was hard against my groin, and I immediately felt a warmth surge through me. Marie's eyes widened as she rolled away. I knew I had to get up quickly. What would Annabelle's mother think of me. We were all laughing when I yelled. "You two don't play fair. I give up. We have got to go if we are going to the old Church, and I do not want Charlie to pee on me."

"We whupped him Marie, Charlie shouted!"

"We sure did," Marie laughed, that'll teach him to mess with us girls, won't it," she said with a wink.

I got up off the floor with Charlie on my back, holding on with her arms around my neck. She was still laughing. We started for the truck and Marie took my arm as we walked. When I got to the truck, I let Charlie slide off my back and asked her to go back and get the blanket, that it might be cold at the old church.

"Ok, but I have to go to the bathroom first."

When Charlie started for the house, Marie whispered to me. "That was fun. Thank you, Zack. It seems like forever since I've Laughed."

"It was fun but I'm afraid that we've left a mess on your porch," I said, looking down at her. She looked the happiest I'd seen her since Annabelle had died. I hoped she was finally inching forward with her life without Annabelle.

"Do not worry about the mess," she said, waving her hand.

I was happy she was laughing again. All storms eventually come to an end. Maybe the sun was about to shine again in Marie's life. I hoped we were finally turning the page to this period of sorrow. I knew that laughter was the enemy of sorrow, and the beginning of happiness, and I felt that Marie's laughter was a positive sign for her and for me.

13

3

The Blacksmith

I DROVE US TO the old First Presbyterian Church on Jefferson Avenue and parked the truck at the end of the sidewalk leading up to the sanctuary. There were no lights on inside, so we sat on the steps and spread the blanket across our knees. We sat there, in silence, for a few minutes, just absorbing the beauty and serenity of this sacred place. Finally, Marie spoke. "Charlie, I know you have something you want to talk to us about. I want you to know that whatever you tell us will be between the three of us. Zack and I love you and would never do anything to hurt you."

Marie then put her arms around Charlie and drew her close. Charlie lay her head against Marie's chest and tears swelled in her eyes. Charlie was silent for a moment, her eyes downcast, and then she spoke.

"Pappy told me once," she said, "if you have a really important decision to make you ought to sleep on it, thinking it through carefully, so that's what I have done."

"And what decisions have you come to?" I asked.

"Two things that I've been studying hard on," she started.

"First, I don't want to be adopted. I don't want to have an asterisk by my name. If Pappy and Momma Calloway adopted Robert, and me, there would always be that asterisk. 'Adopted Daughter, Adopted son.' You see, I can never be your real sister. Calling me sister. Doesn't make it so."

"Secondly, you are part of "your" family. And Robert and I are a family. Nothing we can do to change that. I love Momma Calloway, and I don't want to hurt her, and I know now that I've thought about it that I need to stay there until me and Robert can be on our own. I love Mrs. Marie too and want to stay with her some but I know that I can't do that permanently."

"You know I love you Zack, even when you are being a "Gourd Head." You can never be my real brother, and I'm ok with that. I never want to be far away from you or Mrs. Marie though."

"You will never be an asterisk to me kid, and don't worry, Mrs. Marie and I will never be more than a telephone call away from you, if you need us. I will also see to it that you get to spend plenty of time with Marie."

Once I had made that promise, however, I remembered what Pappy had once told me: "Never make promises too far in the future for events in people's lives change and you may not be able to keep your word. Broken promises may break a person's heart and diminish their trust in you. Pappy said that people who break their word to you are not worthy of your trust any longer. I wasn't sure that was always true, however."

Charlie came to me and threw her arms around my neck and buried her head in my chest, I held her close and kissed her head. Tears swelled in my eyes, Marie looked at me and smiled.

I stood up and said, "It's time to go. Momma will be worried about us. I told her we would be home by 5:30 and it's nearly five now."

We were walking up the sidewalk when a man turned on the sidewalk walking toward us. He wore a battered brown felt hat and a ragged denim jumper. His pants were worn as were his shoes. He walked with a cane; he was a little bent. I figured him to be about the age of my Pappy, maybe a few years older. He reminded me of Mr. Davis, who had been living with us at the time of his death. When he neared us, Marie drew herself closer to me putting her arm around my back. I knew she was frightened even though he was walking on a cane. When we drew near him, he waited for us to approach.

When we were even with him, he said "Excuse me sir, is the church back there open?"

"I don't think so, Sir. No lights on," I said.

"Oh my," he lamented, "I was hoping to find a place to stay for the night and get a bite to eat. I've been without a home for the last two weeks. Oh well," he said, "maybe in the morning I will see if they have any work I can do, and a place to sleep for a few days. I have a brother in Memphis," he continued, "and he has asked me to come and stay with him, until I can get back on my feet. I lost everything I owned in the tornado that hit Rock Hill."

I knew that Rock Hill was just a few miles Southwest of Tupelo, and I had heard about the tornado that had struck the little village; just about destroying the whole community.

"What is your name, sir, if you don't mind me asking? I heard about the storm had hit the little town a few weeks back."

I felt sorry for the man and decided I would offer my help.

"Lukas Robbins," he said offering his hand. "Most folks just call me Luke."

I shook his calloused hand and told him my name. Then I turned toward Marie and said, "This is Mrs. Marie Owens, a good friend of mine, and this," I gestured toward Charlie, she is my sister with an Asterisk." I grinned down at Charlie as her face turned bright red."

The man smiled at Charlie revealing clean white teeth. He had bright blue eyes. I suspected he was a right handsome man if he were cleaned up some, or after a good scrubbing with steel wool and lye soap.

"I don't have much money, but I would be happy to buy you a meal, if you would allow me. "I don't have a place for you to stay, but There's a motel on the edge of town where they advertise rooms for five dollars."

"Son," He said, "I don't have five cents, much less five dollars. I spent the last quarter I had yesterday, for a can of sardines and some cheese, and haven't eaten since. I will accept your generous offer with much gratitude and thanks."

I looked at Marie. She offered no advice and looked astounded that I was even talking to the stranger. He did not seem to be a threat to anyone, he only seemed to be a man who needed a helping hand.

"I tell you what, Mr. Robbins, I just got paid today. Why don't you let me pay for the motel and tomorrow we'll try to figure out how to get you to Memphis. What kind of work did you do, Mr. Robbins?"

"Blacksmith," He said, "welding, horseshoeing and such. Had my own little shop with my living quarters in back. Storm blew it all away along with my tools and two hundred dollars I had saved in a coffee can. All that was left was my big anvil and these clothes on my back, and they're getting a little rank."

I didn't comment on that but, I thought to myself that he was a bit more than a little rank. He smelled worse than a barn stable.

I told him to crawl in the back of the truck if that was agreeable, and I would drive him to the motel. I figured Marie and Charlie would faint dead away if I offered him a seat up front with the rest of us.

"They have a café where you can get a good meal. Things will look better tomorrow," I assured him. "I'll talk to my Pappy and see what we can do to help you get back on your feet. Pappy is good at figuring things out, no matter how difficult the problem might seem."

Lucas crawled in the back of the truck and huddled with his back against the cab. I threw the blanket to him, for the weather had turned much cooler. He wrapped the blanket around his shoulders and pulled his fedora down tight on his head. I loaded into the cab with Marie and Charlie. I stopped at the pay phone in front of the courthouse and called Momma and told her, briefly, what had happened and asked her if she could gather up some old clothes of Pappy's that I could give the man.

Momma said she would see what she could find. "However, you know how your Pappy is, he will not throw away anything until it is fit for nothing but shop rags."

Minutes later, I pulled into our drive. Momma met me with a box full of clothes. She spoke to Lucas when she walked to the truck,

"Hope these fit you Mr. Robbins," she said. "They are a bit worn, but they are clean and maybe they still have a little wear left in them, handing the clothes to him. He stuffed them in his ditty bag that he carried across his shoulder.

"Thank you kindly Maam, hope I can repay you and your son for your generosity."

Momma opened the door and asked Charlie if she wanted to come in. "You need to eat your supper.".".

Charlie resisted. "I want to go with Zack", she said.

Momma hesitated but said OK. "You and Zack hurry back." She did not mention Marie and I wondered what that was all about. I figured she would eventually tell me why she was cool toward Marie.

I drove to the Seven Pines Motel, just across the Natchez Trace Highway, went into the office and rented a room for the night and paid the manager five dollars.

I drove to the end of the motel to the room 110 and opened the door. The room was clean and neatly arranged. It had a television and a phone. Not bad, I thought, for five dollars.

"The café is open until eleven," I said to Lucas, "might want to get a bath and put on some clean clothes before you eat."

"I understand," he said, laughing, "I doubt that they would let me in, the way I look."

I handed him four dollars. "This ought to get you a good meal tonight and breakfast in the morning. I will come by a little after ten in the morning to pick you up and let you meet my Pappy."

I watched Lucas go inside and close the door; He was a beaten man. I climbed in the truck and drove back to Marie's. I got out and opened the door for her. I had the blanket from Mr. Robbins at the motel and now I handed it to Marie.

"You might need to wash that," I said grinning.

"That thing needs to be boiled in lye water for a week," she smiled. Marie looked up at me, her eyes glistening with tears. "Zack," she said, "you beat all. It's no wonder my daughter loved you so. What a kind thing you did for that man." She reached up and gave me a peck on the cheek and a quick hug and turned and hurried inside. I watched until she turned on the lights. I hated to leave her alone.

I drove home with Charlie sitting close beside me. I put my arm around her and pulled her close. "I love you, kiddo. I hope you know that"

"I love you, Brother," she said, "looking up at me, but I wish we were not kin," she said.

"Why would you wish such a thing, Charlie?"

"Then I could marry you!"

"Marry me? You are ten-years old."

"Eleven," she corrected. "Remember I had a birthday.'

"Oh Yeah. I remember," I said grinning.

"I won't always be eleven," she repined, "as I told you before."

"Well, we are kin folk, and, anyway, I could never marry my sister."

"Yeah" she said, "but one of these days I'm gonna make you wish that I was not your sister."

I swallowed hard but I said no more and removed my arm from around her. I didn't want to encourage this girl. I suddenly realized that I loved Charlie and Marie. Perhaps more than I should. One was too old. One was too young to replace the emptiness I felt from losing Annabelle.

My feelings toward Marie, however, was a serious issue. I was only seventeen but there was no doubt that there was something more than friendship going on, but neither of us wanted to admit it and I was not going to be the one to start a conversation about it. Maybe she didn't feel anything. Why should she? Dang, I thought, relationships are hard, and love is blind, so they say.

Lucas Robbins, Blacksmith

*"THERE ARE TIMES THAT STRANGERS
SEEM LIKE FAMILY AND TIMES WHEN
FAMILY SEEMS LIKE STRANGERS."*

Unknown Source

4

Helping A Stranger

AT HOME, MOMMA HAD two plates of food on the table. The
rest of the family had already eaten, and Momma was reading to Robert
Lewis in the ladderback rocker. He was well on his way to dreamworld.

Pappy came in and sat by Charlie at the table and tussled her hair
as he sat down.

"You two been out trying to save the world?" he laughed.

"Yeah," I said. "Just a man who is down on his luck. He got wiped
out by the tornado that hit Rock Hill a few days ago."

"Yeah, I heard about that storm."

Charlie piped up and said, "Zack paid for his room at the motel
and gave him money for food. There were tears in my eyes to see the
man so happy,"

"Guess it was a good thing I got paid today or I couldn't have
been much help to him. I am supposed to go see him tomorrow after
I get out of school and was wondering if you would go with me. I
still have ten dollars so I thought I would buy him a bus ticket to
Memphis." I explained the man's circumstance to Pappy and how the
Tornado destroyed his home and blacksmith shop. Even lost his mule,

his only means of transportation. He said he reckoned he was struck by lightning.

"Tomorrow I'll go with you, and we'll see what we can do to help. Shouldn't be hard to find some work if he knows blacksmithing," Pappy said. "That's a mighty good trade to know."

That night, I thought about the events of the day, but my mind was on Anna. I wondered what she would think of the relationship between her mother and me. I took the Diaries that Marie had given me, and I read the last two entries Anna had made.

January 29, 1958

Dear Diary:

Tomorrow I will leave for Jackson to visit the University of Mississippi School of Medicine. I can't believe my dream of becoming a doctor is finally coming true. All the study and hard work is finally about to pay off. Zack and My mother are going with me. I Love Zack so much for he is going to check into entering Law School at the Mississippi College of Law in Jackson so that we can be married and be together while we are in school.

He is willing to give up his dream of going to the law school at Ole Miss so that I can pursue my dreams. It is no wonder that I love him so. Zack is driving us down, and I hope we can find some time to be together I am very nervous about meeting with the Dean but Zack has a calming effect on me. I pray that all goes well.

January 30, 1958

Dear Diary:

Mother and I spent the day in Jackson on the campus of the University of Mississippi School of Medicine. My dream is finally coming true; to be a doctor. We were given a grand tour of the entire campus, and we had lunch with the Dean of Internal Medicine. Zack had driven us down yesterday and we took the Natchez Trace highway. It was a bit longer route, but it was a beautiful drive. While we toured the campus, Zack toured the State CapitalCapital building and the Jackson law school.

Tonight, we ate at a fine restaurant that had live music and a dance floor. Mom picked up the tab. We got back to the Alumni House Hotel just before midnight. We sat for a while and talked. Zack finally excused himself and went to his room. I had a chance to talk to Mom alone. I told her that I was going to Zacks room and stay the night with him. I told her that I just had a strange feeling that something serious was going to happen and I wanted to be with him. Mother made no attempt to dissuade me but told me to be careful and not to hurt that boy. I promised her I would never intentionally hurt him, for I loved him so.

Zack was shocked when I came to his room but took me in his arms. We made love in the darkness. I stayed until just before dawn when I returned to my room.

I laid the diary aside and turned out the light. Sleep was slow in coming as my mind wrestled with the thoughts of my feelings for Marie Owens and the meeting of Lucas Reynolds.

The next morning, at breakfast we discussed Lucas. I told pappy that he was bent some, that he walked on a cane, but that I thought he was an honest man. "Just seemed like a man looking for a chance to earn a living."

Pappy said, "I know how that feels. I was in the same shape when we moved to Tupelo, a few years ago. Let's go see if there's anything that we can do to help. There is also a chance that he might not want our help, you know. Very often pride keeps people from accepting help when they really need it. That is foolish thinking, for everyone needs a hand up every now and then."

I had not thought of that.

We drove into the Motel parking lot a few minutes later. I parked my truck in front of room 110. Lucas Robbins was sitting in a straight back motel chair outside the door, his bag of personals be*side him.* He was smoking a crooked stem pipe. Me and pappy got out, Lucas stood up when we approached, and I introduced the man to my father.

"Glad to meet you Mr. Robbins," Pappy said, offering his hand.

"Likewise, Luke answered," gripping Pappy's hand firmly.

"Zack here says you've had a little run of bad luck lately and that you were trying to get to Memphis and try to find your brother. He also tells me that you are a blacksmith by trade. I doubt you are gonna find much blacksmithing work in Memphis. Be better off to set up shop here. Plenty of horses and mules to be shod and plow points to sharpen. There's also a shortage of welders too. I believe you will find plenty of customers if you choose to set up shop near Tupelo."

"Mr. Calloway, I don't have a dime to buy new tools to say nothing of building a forge," Lucas stated firmly.

"Well," Pappy said, "we might be able to help you. If you are interested in starting over in the Tupelo area, I have a proposition for you."

"I'd sure like to hear it, for blacksmithing is the only thing I know how to do. I've been at it since I was fourteen. My daddy taught me the trade and left me the little shop when he passed on. The only kin I have is a brother in Memphis who is five years older than me. My mother died giving birth to me. My brother Jack, and pappy raised me the best they could. My dad began teaching me the trade when I was six; he died when I turned fourteen. I never went to any school, but Jack got a little schooling from my momma. We ran the little shop together until I was sixteen, when Jack up and left for Memphis and never came back. Been on my own since then."

"Blacksmithing is an honorable profession, Lucas, and we could sure use one here to serve this area, Pappy stated. My wife and I and our two boys own a farm about five miles out on the highway, and the fellow who owned it before us, had built himself a forge there many years ago, and he had the biggest dang anvil I've ever seen. There's also a petal operated grinding wheel. It's been covered with a tarp for several years I imagine, but if you want to see if it's something you could use, you could be in business. I have four horses and a pair of mules that need shoeing. My neighbor also has a pair of horses that I know need shoeing. If you are interested, we can drive out and look. If you need supplies, we will advance what you need to get things going and when the money comes in, you can pay us back. If you are not interested in that proposition, then Zack will take you to Memphis on Sunday."

Lucas bowed his head and appeared to be thinking hard on Pappy's offer. Finally, he raised his head. "Let's go take a look at that forge, Mr. Calloway." Lucas was silent for several seconds, his eyes downcast. He was obviously thinking about the offer Pappy had made.

We loaded back in my truck and drove to our house to pick up Squat. When we drove into the drive, he met us at the gate with a howl. Momma came out to see what he was howling about, for Squat never howled unless there was a stranger about. I got out and yelled that we were going to the farm and would be back about lunch time. I directed Squat to the back of the truck. He didn't like that one bit. With Pappy sitting up front I guess he thought we were interlopers. His rightful place was beside him in the cab. I had to grab him by the collar and encourage him until he finally gave in and lay down behind the cab. He barked at me when I started to slide into the cab. I didn't know if dogs had a cussing language or not, but if they did, I figured I was getting a royal one right then. We drove out to the farm. When we pulled up to the barn, Joe Webb was standing beside Pappy's black Mare. He had the mare saddled and was ready to mount up when I pulled to a stop beside him. Pappy opened the Door and he and Lucas slid out.

"What's up Joe?" Pappy asked.

"Heard a cow bawling over yonder somewhere. Sounded like a momma cow looking for her calf. Thought I might better ride out and see why she was carrying on so."

Pappy introduced Lucas to Joe and told Joe that he had some business to talk over with him.

"Let Zack Saddle his horse and he can ride with you. You might need some help."

Joe told me to catch my horse and he would get the saddle from inside the barn. I saddled the grey and we rode toward the big pasture over by the highway. It felt good to be riding again, and the Grey seemed to like it too. We rode for nearly a half mile before we spotted the bawling cow. She was walking around and around a blackjack-saw-brier thicket. We rode up to the thicket and dismounted. Joe took a gloved hand and found a place where he could see into the thicket.

"Calf is in there," He announced, "don't know how he got there but the momma cow couldn't get to her baby. And we can't either. Why don't you ride back and get the Machetes from the tool room. We are going to have to cut away some brush. I couldn't tell if the calf was injured, but it looks like he's in a pickle and can't get up."

I rode back to the tool shed behind the barn a grabbed the two machetes, and rode back to the thicket. We went to work slashing away. In a half hour we had cleared a three-foot-wide path to the trapped animal. I knelt beside the calf and rubbed it's back and head.

"He is shivering," I said. "Must have been in here for a while."

"Fear," Joe said. "Common in people and animals. He will stop shaking when we get him to his momma. Fear can cause a person or animal to not be able to move or think clearly."

We lifted the calf carefully from being wedged between two blackjack bushes. Joe stood the calf upright to see if he could walk on his own. He staggered, took a few steps and fell on his side. I picked the calf up and carried it to the open pasture. Momma cow came running to her baby. She didn't look none too friendly. I sat the calf down quickly and ran for my horse. The calf stood on his own and I reach for my horse's saddle horn and launched into the saddle. The calf went straight to its momma for his nourishment. Joe and I rode back to the barn. Pappy and Lucas had apparently completed their business and were sitting on hay bales just outside the barn hall. We unsaddled the horses, rubbed them down and turned them in the horse lot. Joe took the tools to the tool shed and I took the saddles to the tack room. We then joined Pappy and Lucas and grabbed two five-gallon buckets to sit on. Pappy had made coffee and the three men went to the tack room and retrieved cups and returned to the hay bales. Pappy explained to

Joe what had happened to Lucas and that he and I were trying to get him back in business.

"Lucas thinks he can have the forge ready for fire as soon as he can get some coal for fuel."

"What can I do to help?" Joe asked.

"Nothing right now," Pappy said, "but he has to have a place to stay. The tool shed out there is good and tight. With a little work we could turn it into a decent place to sleep. I'll have Allie and Mrs. McCullough to take a look at it and see what they can do with it."

"It won't take much for me. A cot for sleeping and maybe a hot plate for making coffee and such. I can get water from the well."

"He can stay with me for a while," Joe said. "I've got an extra bedroom. Probably need some serious cleaning, and I am not a very good cook either. I'll take him to town whenever he is ready to buy supplies."

Pappy got up from the hay bale and told Lucas that he was going to saddle the black mare and ride out to the thicket and check on the calf and then up to the East pasture.

"We've got thirty or forty head up there that I haven't checked on in a day or two. Won't take long." Joe told Pappy that he would stay and help Lucas get the blacksmith shop cleaned up and take an inventory of things he had and try to figure out what he needed to buy. Me and pappy headed to the horse lot. After about an hour of riding we left the farm and made it back to Tupelo just after one o'clock. Momma made us sandwiches for lunch, and she sat with us at the kitchen table. She seemed like she was happy to see Pappy—as if he had been gone for a week. She was like that about Pappy.

"Got a call from Willie this morning," she said. "His training will be over, and he will be home for Easter. The Air Force is going to send him to school at Ole Miss on a military scholarship. You two won't be staying together though. He will be housed in Military quarters. He will be here for your graduation in May. I'm glad you two will be in school at the same time. Maybe he can keep you out of trouble."

"What? Keep me out of trouble? He's the troublemaker. I'm the good son."

"Humph!" Pappy laughed.

Pappy and I finished our lunch and he asked me to write a small advertisement to put in the Tupelo Journal. He told me, generally, what he wanted to say in the ad. I quickly wrote it out on a sheet of notebook paper.

> *This note is to the folks that live in an around the Rock Hill community on behalf of Mr. Lucas Robbins, who owned and operated a small Blacksmith shop, there for many years. The tornado that hit the town a few weeks ago destroyed the shop and his living quarters. The only thing that he salvaged was a large anvil. He also lost $200.00 and some receipts that he kept in a Gold Mine coffee can. All the small tools and buildings were carried away in the storm. Mr. Robbins asks for your help. If you find blacksmith tools and would like to help, you could drop them off at Joe Webb's place at Route 5, box 503 on Davis Road south of Tupelo. Or you can call and leave a message at TU555. Your help would be appreciated. He's trying to get back in business just south of town.*

We drove to The Journal newspaper office and Pappy went inside and paid for the ad. I wondered if Pappy really thought anyone would return a can with two hundred dollars in it. Pappy thought that most people were honest and generous and would do the right thing. I was a doubting Thomas, but Pappy was an eternal optimist.

Joe and Lucas worked most of the next week getting the shop ready to take on customers. Lucas had bought horseshoes in various lengths and a supply of angle iron and steel. He built racks for everything. Mrs. McCullough, Charlie, and momma painted him a rough sign to hang out on the main highway with an arrow pointing toward the Davis Road. Lucas had ordered a ton of coal and had it dumped right beside the shop. The shop had swinging doors wide enough for a wagon or a pick-up truck to be pulled inside. On Saturday Lucas officially opened for business, and Pappy brought Momma, Robert and Charlie out to watch for a while. Momma, Mrs. McCullough and Charlie worked on getting the tool shop suitable for living quarters. Momma had brought out the cot that Mr. Davis had used when he was living with us, they also brought a wash basin and a small dining table, a pair of ladder back chairs, a rocking chair and, a bedside table with a lamp. Mrs. McCullough brought over a hot plate for cooking. They had also covered the floor with linoleum rug. It was nothing fancy, but it was livable, the walls were tight, and a coal-oil heater would provide plenty of warmth.

Joe Webb surprised us all when he announced that people had dropped off several pieces of blacksmith tools at his place and three Goldmine coffee cans with $200.00 in each can, nothing to identify who sent the money or the tools. They just left it on his porch.

Pappy was right. "You can never overestimate the goodness in people." But I would add. "Or evil".

The blacksmith shop was a fascination to Robert. Pappy put out two bales of hay for him to sit on where he could watch Lucas shoe the horses, heating the shoe and then shaping them on the anvil with shop hammer. Much of the time he sat with his hands covering his ears for the hammer on the anvil was super loud. Charlie showed little interest in the blacksmith shop and spent most of the time on the heels of Momma and Mrs. McCullough.

By noon the three of them had the little tool shop looking almost like a home. When they had finished, Charlie went to Lucas and asked him to come and see how he liked his new room, I was interested in what he would say, so I followed. Charlie took his hand and walked, her mouth running like a steam engine every step of the way. Lucas wore leather chaps and a leather apron. He wore a blue bandana around his neck. He removed the apron but kept the chaps on, and they flopped some as he walked, and he smelled strongly of coal smoke. Lucas had to bend down some as he entered the door for it was only a six-foot door. The surprise on his face was evidence that he liked his new home.

5

New Home for Lucas

"WHAT TWO DO YOU think, Mr. Lucas," Charlie bubbled with excitement as they stepped inside. "Do you like your new place? You've got a table and two chairs. I could, maybe, come and see you sometime if you wanted and I could bring you some books to read." She said without catching a breath.

"I would love it if you would come and visit me some time, Charlie, but I'm sorry to say that I never learned how to read or write. Teardrops forming in the corner of his blue eyes. Don't have any schooling at all. Never have been inside a schoolhouse. I love this place; it is the best place I've ever had. Maybe you could come over on Sunday afternoon and read to me."

I could see that Charlie was shocked to learn that Lucas could not read or write, and I knew the wheels were turning like a spinning Jenny in her pretty head.

"I'd like to do that," Charlie said, looking up at him, her lips quivering. "I read really good and that would be fun. Maybe I could help you learn to read too."

Lucas did not comment, but he knelt beside Charlie and drew the child to himself, with Momma and Mrs. McCullough looking on; both wiping away tears. Lukas clung to the child for a long moment as if he never wanted to let the girl go, I wondered to myself, how long it had been since he had been shown this much love from a child—or from anyone else for that matter. Finally, he stood, tried to straighten his arthritic back, thanked the ladies for their help, doffed his hat, turned and walked out the door. Charlie watched him walk away, but her mind was in another place.

Charlie was an easy child to love, and she returned it easily as well. I felt that love was a special thing when it found its way into a heart that was barren of that feeling. Lucas had a heart that had only known loneliness, sorrow, emptiness, and sadness, I imagined. I was so lucky to never have had those feelings in my heart. I Had people around me who loved me, and I could return the same feelings with joy.

Momma took Pappy's truck and carried Robert and Charlie home just about noontime. I was glad that she did that, for I wanted to talk to Pappy about a serious matter and I didn't want little ears to hear what we were discussing. Pappy and I and squat left the farm an hour later and I drove to where the dirt road met the highway. I pulled over under a big White Oak tree and shut off the engine. I had not planned what I would say, but I was seeking answers to serious questions, and I didn't know where else to go but to Pappy. Pappy seemed to have a special insight into what people were thinking, but rarely offered an opinion unless he was asked.

PICTURE
MARIE OWENS
Full Page

*"LOVE IS LIKE A NOVEL IT CAN BE
EITHER FACT OR FICTION"*

RC

6

Dancing to A Platonic Tune

"WHAT'S UP, SON?"

"Got some questions for you Pap. Hypothetical. Some things on my mind, and I trust your judgement on questions about what is right and wrong about love, marriage, romance and such."

"Hypothetical, huh, big word. I Doubt if I can help you much on hypotheticals Zack but ask away."

"Would you ever marry a woman that was a decade or more older than you?"

Pappy looked down and grinned. "Nope!" I wouldn't he said.

"Mind if I ask why not?"

"Already got a wife he said, remember your Momma?" Pappy grinned.

"Oh yeah, I said but What If you didn't?" I asked.

"Why don't you quit beating around the bushes and give me names?" Pappy said. "Maybe I can help."

"I can't do that. You'd know who I was talking about."

"I'm pretty sure I already know that; You're talking about yourself and Marie Owens, aren't you?"

You could have knocked me down with a squirrel's tail. I knew Pappy was a perceptive person, but I never suspected that I had ever given any signal that there was anything brewing between Marie and me except friendship.

"We are just friends," I said. "She needs me right now and we have become extremely close but nothing romantic, I insisted. A platonic, relationship I reckon you would call it."

"I don't reckon I would call it that because I don't know what it means. Another big word."

"Just means a friendship between a man and a woman. Without romantic feelings."

"I've heard of people trying to dance to that tune before. Friendships between men and women are difficult to dance to. They both, sooner or later, want more. Marie Owens is a beautiful woman son, and she has been through hell, losing both her parents in a boating accident, a husband in the war, and now, a daughter. I figure she is as lost as a blind duck in a snowstorm and she's searching for something to fill the emptiness inside her. It may cause her to want to become more than friends. Don't want you to lose your bearing and do something you may both be sorry for later. I don't think there is anything wrong with a young man marrying an older woman. Not one of us humans can help who we love, and we all need someone to make life worth living. Just be careful. Love like most things is never black and white, but shades of grey. The darker the shade, the stronger our feelings. Even marriage doesn't change that. There are times when love fades a little. There is no such thing as a perfect marriage or a perfect relationship."

Pappy's advice didn't clear up much for me, but I got his meaning. I would be leaving for Ole Miss soon, and maybe that separation would give us time to find a bearing. We left the conversation at that, and I drove on, my mind filled with more questions.

CHARLIE BECOMES A TEACHER

Anyone that thought Charlie wasn't serious about teaching Lucas to read, would have been wrong. She was double dog serious, as Pappy says. She had made her mind up that Lucas needed to be able to read and write, and count, and she was just the one to teach him how. She had Momma take her to the library for First Grade readers and a first-grade arithmetic book. She gathered pencils and paper and notebook. She also took a calendar to help him learn the days of the month and the months of the year, it was a daunting task that she had before her, but she was determined to succeed.

Momma had agreed to allow Charlie to go to visit with Lucas only on Sunday afternoons for two hours, but that was all. She also insisted that another adult go with her through her reading session. The first lesson Charlie invited Marie to go with her and help her if she had problems.

Marie was happy to go with her, and she seemed to enjoy the time she spent with Lucas, she was amazed how bright the man was, and how eager to learn. She was embarrassed at how wrong her first impression of Lucas had been. Zack, she thought, had sensed immediately that there was something special about this homeless man in filthy clothes. Not only was he very bright, but with new clothes, he was right handsome.

After two weeks he had led learned how to count to a hundred and the letters of the alphabet, but still had some trouble with the sounds. Charlie was patient with Lucas and knew just how to get the most out of him. A kiss in his cheek when he did something really difficult worked wonders on Lucas. I had gone along with Charlie and Marie, but Charlie insisted that I did not watch her teach the first lesson.

"You'll make fun of me and how I teach," she said.
"Yeah, you are probably right," I grinned.
"You're evil," she snapped.
"I'm an angel."
"Bull: more likely Lucifer."

Marie said that she had spent about half the time with reading and the second mostly on math. Charlie had planned to use the calendar in the next week's lesson. Charlie was opening a door to a bright new world for Lucas, and he was anxious to push it open wide. At the same time, Charlie was learning to love teaching, and it was something that she came by naturally.

"IF YOU MARRY YOUR ADOPTED SISTER,
YOUR DAUGHTER IS YOUR NIECE."

RC

7

Pappy Gets A Letter

Saturday morning before Easter, Willy called to let us know that he would be flying into Columbus Air Force Base about noon. He asked if I could pick him up at the front gate. I told him that I would be there. He made no mention of Jessica, and I asked no questions. He would tell me what he wanted me to know and nothing more. I knew he loved Jessica but sure didn't want to get kicked by the same mule twice.

Willy was waiting at the front gate when I arrived. He was chatting with the guards when I pulled up to the guard shack. The guard told me to make a U-turn and pick up my passenger on the other side of the guard house, Willy saluted the men and pushed himself in the truck beside me. He had not changed much in the months he had been in flight training. He wore dressed khakis but now had silver wings on his chest. We shook hands, which seemed a little awkward, for I could never remember the two of us doing that before.

"This old truck still running I see," he stated. "Figured it would be in the junk yard by now."

"Now don't be belittling my truck. What are you driving?" I grinned.

"Touché," he replied.

"I saved most of my money while I was in flight training. Going next Monday to see what I can buy for a thousand dollars."

"Pappy will help you get a good deal. He knows just about everybody in town and bought a lot of vehicles when he owned the lumber yard."

"Yeah, I was hoping to get a new chevy truck, but I hear they're selling for two thousand or more now."

"Yeah, too expensive for my checkbook. I'm having a new engine and clutch put in this old heap, and a new paint job. It's going to cost me about two hundred. I'm hoping it will get me through college."

Suddenly, the subject changed when Willy asked me if I had started dating again since Anna died.

It was a fair question; it had been weeks since Anna had died.

"Nope, I haven't given it but very little thought. Anna is still in my heart right now and I can hardly keep from crying when I think about her. I know I need to move on, but it's hard."

"I'm sorry I brought it up brother. I know how much you loved her."

"No problem. How about you? Are you seeing anyone?"

"Well as a matter of fact, Jessie and I have been talking and writing again. I swear I can't get over that girl. She just gets under my skin, and I can't think straight. I am supposed to call her as soon as I get In. Have you seen her or talked to her since I was here before?"

"Sometimes questions that people ask aren't really the real question they want to ask," I thought.

I knew that what Willy was really asking was, "Had I seen her with other boys?"

"I've seen her at school a few times and she asked me about you once. That is all. Saw her and Penelope at the drugstore once. They asked me to join them for a Coke, but I declined. I had an important delivery for the Law Firm. They are both still beautiful. I don't think she is going out with other guys, if that's what you want to know. I think she is still in love with you, although I don't know why."

"Beats me too."

"Maybe the four of us can go out while I'm here," Willy allowed.

"We'll see." I nodded.

We made it to Tupelo just past 1:30 in the afternoon. The air was cool for early spring, and Willy was greeted with arms full of kids as soon as he stepped onto the porch. Robert Lewis in one arm and Charlie on the other. Momma held the front door open and waited her turn. Pappy was standing right behind her. He was smiling like a bear with a honeycomb. Finally, we were all ushered into the living room. Pappy had a small fire going in the fireplace that made the room warm and cozy. After a few minutes Willy went to the phone to call Jessie. We could hear him talking in low tones but couldn't make out what they were saying. Minutes later he asked Momma if it was alright if he asked Jessie to have Easter dinner with us.

"Yes, of course," she said. "We will eat about 5:30. Right now, we have a family matter to discuss. Today we received a letter from the Law Firm in Indianola that was responsible for us having Charlie and Robert as part of our family, Pappy wants the whole family to hear what it says, so we'll go to the dining table, and I will read it so everyone can hear."

We all gathered around the big table, with Robert Lewis sitting on Willy's knees and Charlie on mine. Momma opened the long envelope that Pappy had signed for and began to read.

Roseburg & Associates
Attorneys at Law
2373 North Main
Indianola, Mississippi

April 2, 1953

Mr. AC Calloway
544 Jefferson, Ave. Tupelo,
Mississippi

Dear Mr. and Mrs. Calloway;'

It has been almost two years now since you were awarded custody of the two Children, Charles Russell and Robert Lewis Calloway. From what you have told me on the phone, both are doing very well in their new home, but let me get to the matter about which I am writing.

About four weeks ago, our firm received a letter from a man by the name of Joseph Ledbetter from Chicago Illinois. He claimed that he was a full brother to your cousin Hebert Calloway. He claimed that your cousin was not your cousin at all. His claim was that he and mister Ledbetter had spent two years in prison for armed robbery in Illinois and after they had served their time, Herbert applied to the courts for a name change and it was granted. His name was now Herbert Calloway. Herbert lived the rest of his life an honest man, a good husband and Father to his children. His attorney claimed that Mr. Ledbetter was due part of the estate of Herbert Calloway.

Our firm looked into the matter and found that it was true that Herbert had, in fact, had his name changed. Ledbetter, however, has no claim on the estate since Herbert's last Will and Testament was a legally binding document. I, personally talked with the chancery judge and he promised to write a letter to Mr. Ledbetter's attorney and explain the law to him and tell him that any further interference in this case could possibly lead to criminal charges. This affects nothing with your custody of the children. It just means you were never related to Herbert Calloway, if you have questions, please call. If you happen to be in Indianola, please drop by. I would love to hear more about how the children are progressing.

Sincerely

Melvin Roseberg'

"Zack, what does that letter Mean?" Charlie questioned.

"It means we can give you back; go pack your clothes, I'll put you on a bus," Willy inserted and laughed.

"You are mean," Charlie responded. The military sure hasn't taught you manners. Thought you were supposed to be an officer and a gentleman."

Momma did not think was a bit funny either, and scolded Willy harshly.

Willy turned red faced, and he apologized.

"Nothing will change for you and Robert," Pappy answered. "You will still be our children. It just means we were never kin to your mother and daddy."

"Well, it means a lot more than that to me!" as she turned her head up toward me and smiled but, thank heavens, she didn't comment further.

"Oh God, I thought, I knew what she was thinking."

When momma finished reading the letter, Willy asked Pappy if he could use the truck to go and see Jessie and bring her over for dinner. I told Pappy I was going by the Law firm for a little while but would be back in time for dinner. I did not mention that I was going by to see Marie Owens. Pappy looked at me sideways anyway as if he knew exactly what I was doing. I had received my graduation invitations that week and wanted to make sure everyone at the law firm received an invitation, so I was going to deliver them in person. This being Saturday, however, I would likely not catch the whole crew. Although Saturday was the firm's busiest day of the week, Mr. Webb let the staff go early if he could.

I took my box of cards, each with a small picture of me in my cap and gown. I parked in front and took the steps up to the second floor. Only Mr. Webb and his Secretary, Audrey Free, were still working. Mrs. Free was filing the last of the work for the day. I gave her the signed card with a written thank you for her kindness.

"When will you be off to the University?" She asked, as I turned to go back to Mr. Webb's Office.

"I'm going to move in my apartment the first of May, but I'll not start classes until the 10th

"Well, you have a good time!" she told me.

"I'm gonna try," I said as I stepped into the hallway.

I rapped on Mr. Webb's door.

From inside Mr. Webb's voice boomed. "If you're selling Insurance. I don't want any. If it's whisky or Cigars, I'll take a truck load." I opened the door and went in.

"Rough Day?" I asked as I took his hand.

"Yeah, Zack, seems as if half the people in this town are getting divorced or going bankrupt, or both. I'm sure there must be a relationship there somewhere. I don't like doing business with either one. They sure don't pay the bills. If they're filing for bankruptcy, they don't have money to pay, and if they're getting divorced, they're likely leaving town and you'll never see them again. I can't wait till you get your license and start helping take the load off. What are you doing out today? I thought I gave you the day off. I heard you talking to Mrs. Free up front. What's up?"

"Just wanted to bring you a graduation invitation in person. Hope you can come."

"Wouldn't miss it for the world. Are you making a speech?"

"Short one," I grinned.

"Best Kind," He laughed. Most people don't come to graduations to hear speeches, they are just there to see their son or daughter get that diploma."

I gave him an invitation, and said goodbye, and bid goodbye to Mrs. Free as I walked through the receptionist area and down the stairs to the street. I started my truck and drove to Marie Owen's house, walked up and rapped on the door. Seconds later Marie opened the door. Wearing white pedal pushers and a black pull over. She was a beautiful woman, no matter what she wore. She smiled and nodded with her head for me to come inside.

"What a nice surprise," she said. "Figured you would be with your family all weekend, since your brother is home."

"Just wanted to see you for a few minutes and see what you were doing for Easter."

"My in-laws are coming up in the morning from Columbus, and I've baked a turkey for lunch tomorrow, and they are staying over until

Monday morning. Would you like a Coke or something to drink?" She asked.

"Well, I would take a coke, if you don't mind."

She led me to the dining table and went to the fridge, retrieved two Cokes and sat down cattycornered from me at the end of the table.

"I can tell that there is something on your mind, Zack, so out with it," she laughed.

"I may be out of line by asking this, but I've been wondering. Have you thought about dating again? I know it is probably none of my business, but it has been on my mind since Anna died."

Marie's faced turned red as she squirmed a little in her chair, her eyes cast downward.

"It's not out of line at all, after all, I consider you my very best friend, and the answer is yes, I have thought about it, but I have not acted on those thoughts. How would **you** feel about it if I started going out?"

The question was not what I was anticipating, I turned my eyes away to avoid looking directly at Marie, and really thought about how to answer. The word didn't come easy but there it was.

"How would I feel if you went out with someone? I repeated the question aloud and then I answered. "Jealous," and I knew my face was red.

There was silence for a minute.

"Jealous?" She questioned." Why?"

"I'm not sure I can answer that, but that's what I would feel. Stupid, isn't It?"

"I don't think it's stupid, and I will tell you this; I will not start going out until you approve. I'm afraid we have come so close since Anna's death and we need to talk about our relationship, because I think we are both having feelings that maybe we shouldn't. Does it make any sense to you Zack?"

"Yes, it makes sense, but I feel what I feel, and I don't want to do anything stupid that would embarrass you in a way that would affect our friendship."

"I have worried about it too and I feel the same. I think about it all the time, wondering how we can be friends and nothing more. I wonder if it's possible. You are eighteen and I'm thirty-three and that makes a huge difference with most people."

"Pappy said that platonic relationships are hard tunes to dance to, and I think he is right about that. I loved your daughter so much that I never thought I would ever feel love like that again. I have wondered too what she would think about my feelings toward you. For some reason I feel a little guilty about the matter, and I don't really want to. If I love someone, I do not want to hide it. I want everyone to know how I feel."

"I know." She said, "You are going to be leaving for college soon. Maybe that will give us some time to think this through. And in a way I'm not sure how I feel about your leaving. It feels as if a part of me is being torn away. A part that I can never get back."

So, there it was. She had the same feelings that I was having. I finished my coke and got up to leave. She stood and walked me toward the door and then caught my arm and hugged me tight. There were tears in her eyes now. I returned the embrace and kissed her on the forehead and then broke the embrace, said goodbye, opened the door and ran for my truck. I did not want to see her tears. I Really understood now what Pappy meant about platonic relationships. He was right; I wanted more!

I drove home to find Willy and Jessica sitting together in the front-porch swing. Squat was under the swing as close to Willy as he could get. I pulled one of the ladderback rockers over close and sat down. "What are you two love birds doing?"

"Just swinging, waiting for momma to call us to eat. Guess we are waiting for Bonnie and Doctor Little; they are eating with us tonight. Pappy invited them. He will be glad to see the doctor," Willy surmised. "They enjoy jerking each other's chain."

"Momma will enjoy Bonnie too. She hasn't seen much of her since She and the Doctor moved into his place out on the lake."

Soon they drove into the yard in a brand-new Oldsmobile Ninety-eight. It accepted all the space on the front curb.

"Y'all come on in. Momma and Pappy have been waiting on you. Pappy can't wait to harass the Doctor," I said, as they walked up on the porch. Squat came out to greet Bonnie. She patted him on the head, rubbed his back. He turned to give The Doctor a sniff and went back to his perch beneath the swing.

"Jessie, I haven't seen much of you and Penelope lately? Y'all still pals?" I asked.

"Oh yeah," she said, "but we both have jobs and don't get to hang out together very much. We mostly talk on the phone or at lunch sometimes," she continued. "Work affords us little time for visiting."

"Since you mentioned Penelope, Willy inserted, we were wondering if you might ask her if she would like to go with us out to the big pond and roast wieners and marsh mellows, one night this week?"

"I don't know about that. I have hardly spoken to her since Anna's funeral.:

"All the more reason to ask her to go. Willy said.

"Yes, Jessie inserted, I know that she really likes you, but she is too shy to call you. She was Anna's best friend. The one she confided in about everything. She told me that she liked Naught McCullough a lot, but nothing close to love. She told him how she felt, and she thinks that was why he left school early a joined the Marines.

I don't think she was the reason he joined the Marines. He had been thinking on that for some time. "I tell you what, I will call her tonight and see what her plans are for this week and invite her to go with us. All she can do is say no. Right?"

I immediately felt like I was betraying Marie Owens. I had no deep feelings for Penelope, but I felt a guilt, nonetheless.

Momma called us to supper, and we gathered around the big table. With Willy at home, it seemed like old times. He seemed happy and appeared that whatever differences he and Jessica had was now resolved. Now I wondered what I was going to tell Marie. It seemed that I had dug myself a hole and I couldn't seem to quit digging.

I called Penelope after we had eaten, and everyone had moved out to the front porch. Willy and Jessie, of course, wanted to be alone so the left to drive around town. Charlie and Robert begged to go along with them, but Momma stated a flat no.

"You two have hung on Willy all day, and he needs some time with Jessie." I finally got a few minutes of privacy to call Penny. She answered on the second ring.

"Penny, this is Zack Calloway, how have you been. I have not seen much of you since Anna's funeral."

"Well, what a nice surprise, and I have been working at the City Library after school and haven't had much time to socialize. I know that you were also working after school. I would sometimes see you in your old truck driving around town, I wanted to call and see how you were doing, but I have just not been able to talk to anyone about Anna without crying like a baby. How are you doing. I know how much you loved her, and I know how she loved you. I feel as if a part of my heart has been torn out of me. She had been my best friend forever."

I know how you feel. I'm trying to move on, but the grief is so strong that I just don't have a moment that I'm not thinking about her, The reason I called, is on a lighter subject. My brother Willy is home from the Air force flight training and he and Jessie were wanting to go out to the big pond on our farm, roast wieners, marshmallows and just talk. I was wondering if you would go with me. We were thinking about Wednesday night. It's a great place for us all to get reacquainted after all that's happened."

There were a few seconds of silence, and I was wondering if she had fainted or something, then she answered.

"'Yes, I would love to go, it sounds like fun. What do I need to bring?"

"Just yourself." Bring a jacket, though. It gets cool out there by the pond. I will pick you up at 7:00. Do you still live out by the Baptist Church?

"Yes, how did you know?"

"I delivered some roofing shingles for your dad back when Pappy owned the lumber yard. I am really glad you are coming. I had wanted to talk to you but didn't know how you would feel about that."

"Yeah, she said, for some reason it feels a little awkward when really it shouldn't."

"No, I said it shouldn't, but I know what you mean."

"I will see you Wednesday."

I had no romantic feelings for Penny, but I found myself really looking forward to being with her. Penny was a beautiful girl, like Anna and Jessie. She was more introverted than Anna and Jessica, but she was verry bright and witty when she got to know you.

49

Willy and I drove out to the farm Wednesday afternoon, and hauled some firewood that I had stacked in the woodshed several years before for Mr. Davis. We hauled it down to the pond Levy along with two bales of hay for us to sit on. We picked up Pappy's Coca Cola ice chest to get Ice and cold drinks. We bought marshmallows, wiener, buns and paper napkins, mustard and relish. Willy joked that we had enough food to feed the Tupelo National Guard for two weeks.

Penny called about noon and told me she would be at Jessie's; I was to pick her up there. We picked the girls up just before seven. Both girls wore jeans and white shirts with the collars turned up.

They wore the latest fashion in shoes, black and white loafers. Jessica also brought along her portable transistor radio. The girls were waiting for us sitting on the steps to the front porch. They held jackets across their knees. I shut off the engine and met Penny half-way to the porch. I took her hand and led her to the truck and let her slide in. Her knees were pressing against the gear shift. Jessie and Willy were on the passenger side. We rolled the windows down for it was still a very warm day. The sun was setting below the pines on the far ridge when we approached the pond. The sun reflecting its last rays across the waters when we drove onto the levy.

"What a beautiful place," Penny exclaimed. Are there fish in this pond?"

"You bet." Some big ones too; Catfish and Brim, and some Crappie."

"I love to fish, she said. My dad used to take me and Mom over at the big lake."

"Really? I said looking at her sideways."

"What? She said, you look surprised."

"Just didn't picture you baiting a hook, you're so pretty and all."

She laughed; you might be surprised at what I like to do."

"Well, I'm looking forward to finding out.

"Well, would you like for me to bring you to fish some afternoon. We've got plenty of fishing gear in the woodshed."

I've got my own gear, but yes, I'd like to come fishing with you. You better be prepared to get beat on me catching fish though. She turned head sideways and smiled and did that thing with her eyes that sends chills up a guy's back. I think all girls are born with that eye thing. Penny had it mastered.

"OK I said, Let's make it soon, for graduation is coming soon."

"How about next week, she asked. I get off early on Wednesday and Saturday."

"Let's make it Wednesday. The law firm is closed on Wednesday afternoons."

"Sounds good she said. And added, I noticed you have horses. I like to ride."

"Well, we can do that tonight. If you'd like."

"Oh, yes, can we?" she said smiling."

"Sure, let's get the fire going and I'll saddle the black for you. I'll ride the grey." The black mare is very gentle and the grey, not so much, but she likes me."

"While Willy and Jessie were unloading the truck, Penny and I set about getting the fire started. I was amazed at how she was acquainted with the outdoors. I knew I was going to like this girl. We got the fire going and Penny walked with me to the horse lot and helped me saddle the Black and the Grey.

"We call the Mare Lady, I said.

"Oh, how original," she laughed, and did the thing with her eyes again. "The grey here is Sparky. The tan over there is Dusty" The red over there we call, can you guess? Yeah, we call her Red"

The stirrups were a little long for her, so I quickly adjusted them. We rode back to the pond and asked Willy and Jesse if they wanted to catch the other horses and go with us. Jessie said no that she didn't ride. I knew that Willy would like to saddle up but said nothing. I knew too that the two needed some time for just the two of them. Penny and I rode toward the back gate to the big pasture along the main highway. She handled the mare with ease, and she really looked good in the saddle. We rode down to the pasture where Joe fed the cattle and they gathered in a herd when we approached.

"Can I pet the baby calves?" she asked.

I dismounted and went over to help with the smallest calf. White faced cattle are normally a gentle breed and the mother cow let Penny rub her all over and the calf didn't mind either since he was nursing.

"How pretty she said, I love baby calves,."

"So do I. I was watching her closely so that the other cattle didn't crush her trying to get some of the corn."

We better move along, before we get trampled on. I took her hand and pulled her to me and opened the gate. I told her I wanted to show her something.

"What? She asked."

"Got to show you I said, as I gave her a boost into the saddle, mounted and she rode alongside me to the ridge overlooking the meadow where the cattle were fenced. I stopped atop the ridge beneath a large White Oak. "What do you think?"

"It's beautiful up here she said."

"Yes, it is. I mean to build a house right here after I finish law school. This will be my home. Pappy deeded me four hundred acres and Willy the same. Don't know what his plans are but I want to have cattle and horses. I can't wait to have a place of my own,"

"Why are you telling me this?" she asked."

"Don't know for sure. It just felt right. I hope you don't mind. I never got the chance to show Anna, but I don't think she would have ever given in to moving out of the city."

"No, I don't mind at all. Anna was my best friend, but I'm not Anna!"

"You know, we're going to be graduating in a few weeks and I haven't even asked you what your plans are."

"It has been my plan for years, to be a teacher, I love children and I think I will be happy doing that, I plan to attend college at the "W" in Columbus."

"The "W?"

"Yes, Mississippi State College for Women."

"Didn't know there was a school in Columbus."

"Well now you do, she said.: What do you think."

"I think you'll make a great teacher. I'm disappointed you will not be going to Ole Miss."

Better be getting back, I said. Willy will be starved and ready to eat. That boy eats like a horse and never gains an ounce. "I have sure enjoyed our ride and our talk. I hope I haven't bored you to death."

"No, I have loved it and hope we can come out here again before we go off to school."

"I will make sure that happens."

"We rode back to the barn, to turn the horses to the lot. Lucas heard us and came out. I introduced him to Penny and told him what we were planning for the evening.'

"Sounds like fun. You two go on and I'll tend to the horses."

"Thanks, I said, handing him the reins."

I took Penny's hand, and she didn't seem to mind, and then she put her arm inside and pulled herself close as we walked. I didn't understand my feelings toward her, but I liked what I felt. I wondered how I was going to tell Marie.

We cooked wieners over the open fire and roasted marshmallows, laughed and talked until nearly eleven, when the girls said they had to go. They had promised to be home by midnight. It had been a great night and I had made a new friend,

*"IT MIGHT LOOK LIKE I'M PAYING ATTENTION
BUT, IN MY HEAD, I'M DREAMING ABOUT
A NEW CHEVY PICKUP WITH A GOOD
RADIO AND AIR CONDITIONING."*

Robert Coleman

8

Kicking Tires

"MONDAY MORNING PAPPY AND Willy went to look for Willy a truck at the Chevrolet dealership. I still had school to deal with and my job at the law firm. The firm was not very busy, and Mr. Webb told me I could take the evening off and spend some time with Willy. I drove down to the Chevy dealership on Main Street, and they were still there kicking tires. I parked my truck and walked over. The owner of the place knew Pappy well, and due to his respect for Pappy was managing the sale instead of one of their salespeople. I knew him from my job at the law firm. I was in his office at least three times a week. When he saw me, he roared, "Oh good heavens, not another Calloway to bargain with. I already feel like I've been skinned and gutted by these two. I feel like I ought to just give them the dang truck so I could get on with trying to make a living.

Willy was looking at a new truck, which was a last year's model, it was a sharp truck with a chrome grill and whitewall tires a radio and a heater. Willy called me aside and told me that then dealer had offered to sell it for a thousand dollars and would finance the balance, but Pappy would not agree to the financing, and I've only got six hundred that I can afford to spend.

"You have a problem, don't you?"

I looked the truck over and asked if that was the truck he wanted. He said it was.

"I tell you what, I'll let you have the four hundred."

"Where in heaven's name did you get that kind of money? You been robbing old ladies?"

"I'd been saving every cent I could get my hands on, for me and Anna were planning to get married when school was out. Don't need the money now."

"I can pay you back a little each month when I get my stipend from the Air Force. But brother, that won't be until June."

"No payback necessary, Willy. It's a gift. Go get the paperwork while I run to the bank. Be back in a few minutes,"

"I started walking toward my truck, and I heard him tell Mr. Ship, I'll take it. A huge smile came across Mr. Ships face,

"Alright! He laughed. That's a smart boy you've raised there, it will take me a few minutes to get the financing papers ready."

"Won't need any financing. I'll pay cash."

"Fine, he said, I'll have the crew wash and clean it up and fill your tank with gas. It'll take about an hour. You can wait or come back in an hour, and It will be ready."

"It's about lunch time," Willy said. "I think we'll go to the drug store and get a burger if I can get Pappy to pay, since I told him I felt like I'd been robbed by Jessie James."

Pappy was shaking his head, Willy told me later. He couldn't figure Just what happened. I drove up just as Willy and Pappy were shaking hands with Mr. Ship to leave. I followed them over to the drugstore and Willy was a happy man, Pappy was dumbfounded, and I was now as poor as Joe's turkey. But I was happy too. I ate my burger and left Pappy and willy at the Drugstore talking about Willy's new wheels. I drove to Marie Owens and pulled into the drive just before one o'clock. She was sitting in the swing darning a pair of Jeans. She motioned for me to come and sit. She laid her darning aside and asked if I would like a glass of fresh lemonade.

"Yes, if you don't mind."

She left for a minute to retrieve the cold lemonade.

"I've been with Willy to buy himself a new truck. "He bought himself a new Chevy—very sharp. I thought about trying to get a new one before I started to school but didn't want to go into debt. I'm getting a new motor put in mine and a new paint job for a hundred and fifty dollars. Got a few other things I want to have done to it. Luke Barns, down at the Western Auto is putting me a new radio and new heater core for fifty dollars; Hope it will get me through school."

"I'm sure you'll find a way to keep it running."

We made small talk for a while and then she dropped a bomb on me.

"Do you remember the detective from the State Police, Gene Edwards, when he was working the case where that young doctor, Jason Wilbanks killed himself?"

"Yes, I remember him all too well. He and his partner came by the lumber yard and questioned me. I didn't know much to tell them."

"Well, he has stopped by a couple of times to see how I was doing. To make a long story short, he stopped by yesterday and asked me out to dinner, and I said I would think about it over the night and let him know. I wanted to talk with you before I gave him an answer. It was probably a mistake, and I don't want to hurt you, but I felt we are just getting in too deep for our own good. Are you angry?"

"No, I don't think I could ever be angry at you. But the J-word is still there."

"I know.," she said, "and I feel like I'm betraying you.'"

"What I want most for you, Marie, is for you to find happiness and find someone you can share your life with, and I am not a very good candidate. I'm getting ready to go off to college and I will be in school for at least six years. I don't expect I'll be able to have much of a relationship with anyone during that time and I know you need someone that can give you the love and attention you deserve. I still want to see you when I can, and I hope that won't change for a while. You can come to Oxford some too, I hope."

"Well, she said, let's just see how it goes. I haven't had a date in seventeen years", she laughed. "That's awful. He seems like a really nice man though and really smart."

"I am sure he is, or you wouldn't be worried about it." I didn't mention anything about Penelope and our cook-out at the pond. I didn't want to be the one to break up our relationship. I got up to leave and told her I was going to meet Willy to try out his new truck. We embraced and I held her tight for just a minute too long. I felt the warmth running through us both.

"Are you sure that you're ok with this?" She asked.

"No, I'm not. But I think you need to try this and see how it works out. You are never going to know until you give it an honest try."

"WHAT WE ARE IS GOD'S GIFT TO US.
WHAT WE BECOME IS OUR GIFT TO GOD."

Eleanor Bacon

9

Honors for Anna

THE END OF SCHOOL came quickly, I had earned the honor of Valedictorian with the highest grade through the four years of High school. However, I asked the class and staff to bestow that honor on Annabel Owens, since her grades had been the highest at the time of her death and I asked if I could give a short speech in her honor. The class and teachers and administrators agreed that it would be appropriate.

Each graduate was allotted 8 tickets for family and friends. The High School auditorium seated five hundred and there were folding chairs added to seat another two hundred. The place was packed. There was no air conditioning, so by the time the ceremony began it was well over a hundred degrees inside. My family only needed five tickets, but I made sure Mr. Webb and his wife got tickets.

Marie Owens gave me her extra tickets and I gave tickets to Joe Webb and Mrs. McCullough and at the request of Charlie. My last ticket went to Lucas Robins, and I asked Marie if she would escort Lucas and she seemed happy I asked. Doctor little had also asked to say a few words about Anna, and he was seated on the stage with Administrators. There were 108 Seniors in the Class of '58–the largest class in the history of the school. Pappy and Momma, Willy, Charlie and Robert Lewis sat with Marie, Lucas and Bonnie Little on the front row.

I had never spoke to a large group before, so I was nervous when I stepped up to the podium.

"To the graduating class of 1958, I would like to say to the students, the teachers, the administrators, and especially to the parents, thank you for being here tonight. For those of you that don't know me, I am Zack Calloway," I began.

"I have been given the honor of accepting the Valedictorian's award for Annabelle Owens who held the highest-grade point average for the four years of high school. There were four of us that were tied for the honor, but the class voted that Annabelle should receive the award.

A placard in Anna's Honor will be placed on the Wall of Honor at the entrance to the High School. As most of the students already know, Anna and I had been sweethearts since I met her when my moved here to Tupelo from Big Flat a little over six years ago. What they did not know was that we planned to be married in June after graduation. I had asked her to marry me just weeks before the tragic accident that took Anna's life.

Anna planned to be a doctor and she dedicated any spare time she had working at the Medical Center for Doctor Little. Anna's passion for medicine didn't leave much time for romance, but I loved her more than any person on this earth. Anna died as most of you know, trying to save a child. She once told me that she believed that God had a special cause for us. We couldn't have imagined that she would die saving a child's life.

I would encourage each of my fellow students to pursue whatever you choose to do in life, pursue it with a passion and as vigorously as Annabelle did. In closing, I would like to tell you all this: Anna loved Tupelo. She loved the town and its people. She called Tupelo her town. She wanted to practice medicine right here in Tupelo. I will always think of it as Anna's Town. Thank you all again for coming. Your presence shows us that you care for us as Anna cared for you."

I sat down as Dr. little spoke about Anna's dedication and passion for medicine and her love of children. He was a gifted and eloquent speaker. There were many tears shed before he was through speaking. The high school principal then proceeded to hand out diplomas to the one hundred and eight seniors.

After the ceremony, Pappy took the family to dinner at the Natchez Trace Inn, as he had done a year before with Willy. I asked Marie if she would like to join us and she said no that she had invited Lukas to her house for coffee and pie, but she thanked me for inviting her.

Willy wanted me to ask Penny, but she was having dinner with her family. She didn't say where. Doctor Little and Bonnie did come along. He and Pappy acted like teenagers, poking fun at each other. Finally, Momma scolded Pappy, saying, "These folks will think you two are bitter enemies." I could tell, however, that Momma was enjoying the banter as much as pappy.

Finally, they brought our food and the place got quite as we ate the best fried chicken, I think I had ever eaten. Willy and Jessie were the first to finish their meal and asked to be excused. It was a great time with family, and everyone was happy. Doctor Little and Bonnie gave me a card with a hundred dollars. I was shocked at their generosity. I then shook the doctor's hand and thanked him, and I gave Miss Bonnie a hug. The Doctor was a wealthy man, and so was Bonnie. They were the kind of folks that when you talked to them, you might think that they didn't have two dimes to rub together. I knew, however. that there was no one more generous to those less fortunate, than the Doctor and Ms. Bonnie.

After Wayne had died Bonnie and the doctor drew closer to Momma and Pappy and that helped to ease the sorrow that Pappy felt from losing his old friend. The doctor was the same age as Pappy, but that was about all they had in common. Doctor Little was an educated man and Pappy had little schooling, but the friendship grew, and Doctor Little often sought Pappy's advice on how to deal with a whole range of problems. Pappy was not educated, but he was a very smart man.

*"WHEN I DIE JUST LAY ME DOWN, SOMEWHERE
CLOSE TO THAT OLD TOWN, WHERE THE WHITE
OAKS AND THE WILLOWS WEEP, O'ER THE
TOWN WHERE WILLIAM FAULKNER SLEEPS."*

ROBERT COLEMAN

10

School at The University of Mississippi

ON MAY 1ST, 1958, Willy and I said goodbye to Mom and Pappy, Charlie and Robert Lewis in the driveway to our home in Tupelo and took highway 6 west toward Oxford at mid-morning. Willy was in his brand-new Chevy Pickup truck, and me in my 1940 model Chevy that I had inherited from Mr. Davis four years past. It had a newly rebuilt engine, and a new paint job. I also had a newly installed Motorola radio with twin speakers. I had the volume turned up and the dial set on a Memphis station that played the latest in Rock-and-Roll music. When I turned onto the main highway, Fats Domino was wailing "Blueberry Hill." I could see Willy's truck up ahead of me and wondered what he was listening to. He generally preferred Pure Country. It was a hot day, and I had the windows rolled down and the old truck was cruising easily at fifty-five miles per hour. I pulled out my fifty-cent pair of sunglasses slipped them on and wondered how cool I looked like the scenery flew by. It was a good day.

The day before I had said farewell to Marie Owens. Marie had cried as we embraced and told me she would miss me and wanted me to call and let her know when I had settled into my new place in Oxford. It was a beautiful old town with stately old mansions and Magnolia and White Oak trees that lined many old streets. It was often referred to as Faulkner's town where William Faulkner, the famous writer made his home.

Pappy had introduced Willy and me to the man that he had known for many years. Pappy would often engage the man in a game if checkers on the courthouse square when in town on Saturday afternoons. He just said, "Boys this is Mr. Faulkner, he writes books."

I had never read one of his books all through school, but I intended to make it a point to do so.

I took University Avenue through the Town of Oxford crossing over Lamar Avenue at the top of the long hill and through a canopy of giant Oaks, crossing the railroad bridge that said Hello to Ole Miss. I turned left at the top of the grove and pulled into a parking slot in front of the newly constructed Alumni Hotel and Grill; a pre-determined place for having lunch.

Willy had parked two slots down. We went into the grill and ordered burgers and fries and vanilla shakes. An hour later we parted ways and I drove to my apartment back up University Avenue. I pulled into the drive and cut the engine but left the radio playing Chuck Berry's "Maybelline." I sat and contemplated just what lay ahead for me. If all worked out as planned, I would be here for six years—maybe longer. When the song had finished, I began unloading the clothes and what few possessions I owned.

I suddenly realized that I had no food in the house, and this being Sunday, I would not likely find a store open. However, I drove around the Square of Oxford, and down several side streets, and finally located a 24-hour market that sold gasoline and a few basic provisions. I bought a gallon of milk, a loaf of bread, peanut butter, a jar of grape jelly, cereal and a six pack of Cokes. I would get more on Monday. Oxford was pretty much a dead town on Sundays. The two theaters were open, of course, but not much else.

I made another loop around the Square. Noting the Confederate soldier's statue standing guard in front of the beautiful and stately old courthouse, and Nelson's Department store. I was thoroughly familiar with Oxford. In the fall we had our cotton ginned here at Brown's gin. Pappy would sometimes let us ride to the gin with him. If there was a long waiting line, he would take us to Winter's department store. Winters had a small grill in the back of the store where we could order hot dogs if Pappy was feeling generous. I wondered why it was called the Square. When it was actually a circle. Oh well, I had six years to have that explained to me. Back at the apartment I stowed my purchases in an old International Harvester refrigerator, complements of the apartment owners. I then checked the phone to see if it was working. It was. Momma had issued orders for Willy and me to call home as soon as we were settled. I decided to wait about calling home and called Willy instead.

"You unpacked yet, I asked as Willy answered."

"Yep, he said, but got no food. You?"

"Got milk bread, peanut butter, jelly. All the necessities of life. You want to join me for dinner?"

"Sure, I'll be over by five."

Pappy had bought us each an RCA 19" television the week before we left for school, I could pick up three stations with the Rabbit ears that came with the television, although they were very snowy. Pappy had given us both a strict warning about the televisions; "if your grades are not good, I WILL REPOSESS," he said sternly! we knew he meant business.

Willy arrived at five and we just made sandwiches and drank milk until half the milk was gone. Willy wanted more milk, but I refused. I said we had to save some milk for breakfast. I told him he could have Ice water, but he refused. He helped himself to a Coke, however. Willy stayed until seven o'clock when a rerun of the Gunsmoke western show came on and we watched the show and talked about our plans for the next week, and he left for his room in the dorm.

I turned back the covers of my bed at ten o'clock crawled in and took the phone with me. I took a chance and dialed Penelope's number. I just wanted to tell her that I was settled into my new apartment but ended up talking for twenty minutes. It was good to hear her voice,

"I hope it's not too late to be calling."

"No, No, it's not too late at all, I was getting ready for bed, but I do have my own private phone now. Daddy makes me pay my own phone bill, but I really don't mind. I think it's worth the privacy I have, and I don't tie up the line of Pops.

We argued about it, of course, but he's really just a big push over and he finally agreed. My dad is great. He works really hard all the time, but he always has time for me. I love him dearly. What's going on with you?" she asked.

"Just getting settled for Summer School, I said, but wanted to see if you would be interested in a movie, Saturday night. I enjoyed our time together out at the farm and wanted to see if you felt the same."

"Sure, she said, I would love to go."

"I hate to admit it, but I've been hoping you would call me. I know I can never take the place of Anna, and will not even try, but I like spending time with you. I have always thought you were a really great guy."

"Thank you, Penny, I kind of needed that."

We talked for another fifteen minutes and finally said goodnight. 'I then called Marie Owens. I didn't worry much about the hour, for I knew she would still be up. She had told me that she rarely went to bed before eleven. She told me also that she had signed up for accounting classes at the Ole Miss Extension in Tupelo, and she wanted to earn her CPA license. She said she also had plans to sue the trucking company that had killed her daughter. This was the first time she had mentioned a lawsuit against the trucking company. She really wanted me to oversee the lawsuit when I had passed the bar exam. She said she had been thinking of a way to get access to the records and she needed a CPA license to execute the plan.

I said, "That sounds very interesting," but that was five or six years away.

"There's no big hurry," she said. "I want the Webb firm in Tupelo to manage the suit, and if Mr. Webb agrees we will file suit just before the deadline expires, which is nearly three years away. We will talk more about it when you have some time. I have recently learned of some interesting information that has come to light about the driver of the truck."

Marie definitely had my attention. What kind of information did she have, and how did she come by the information? I was sure Mr. Webb would certainly be interested, but she needed to talk to him quickly. The limitation for filing a wrongful death lawsuit in Mississippi, I was certain was three years and four months of that had already passed. I could certainly help with the lawsuit, but Mr. Webb would have to handle all the heavy lifting. I told her we needed to discuss this as soon as possible if she wanted Mr. Webb to manage her case. She agreed that we needed to talk, but she wasn't ready to divulge any source to anyone but me. She did not want to take a chance that the person that was the source of the information would be compromised.

I went to sleep thinking of Marie Owens, Charlie, and Penelope. It was a ragged sleep, for I realized I cared tremendously for all three. I had forgotten to call home and check in with Momma and Pappy. They would not be happy.

Monday morning, I called Willy to see if he wanted to come by for cereal. He said he was going to the cafeteria. They were opening for the session since students were already settling for the summer. I ate my cereal and finished off the milk with a peanut butter sandwich. At eight, I went to the Bursar's office to pay fees and get a parking permit for the truck. I had earned plenty of scholarship money for my four years of undergraduate work, with some cash left over for incidentals. The Purnell and Calloway lumber Company had set aside a scholarship fund for the children of employees. Willy and I each received fifteen hundred per school year in cash. This and other smaller awards gave me a fat bank account. At least I considered it fat. We did have to maintain a grade point of 3.5.

I finished my tasks by noon and decided to have lunch at the cafeteria with Willy. Then I would call home and take my berating from Momma for not calling. I would then register for my summer school classes. It was my intent to take nine hours each summer semester and then begin a full schedule of eighteen hours each semester, summer and Fall.

By mid-afternoon I had registered for my classes and talked to my assigned adviser, who was also a professor of English Literature. I signed up for his freshman class. English 101 and Algebra I, and I was set. All my classes were on Monday, Wednesday and Friday, leaving time for study and recreation. Willy wanted me to sign up for ROTC on campus. With my grades he assured me I would be accepted. I told him I would sleep on it. With the Draft looming over my head as soon as I graduated, it was worth considering spending a few hours a week on Military Science. I had to make up my mind by Wednesday when registration was to be closed.

I stopped at the bookstore picked up the books I would need for the classes, put down a hundred dollars for the books and another ten dollars for tee shirts for Charlie and Robert Lewis, a scarf for Momma and a cap for Pappy. I doubted he would ever put it on because he liked hats. He had become partial to western style felt with narrow brims. Pappy's habits were hard to change. He had started wearing western boots and that was at Joe Webb's urging. He had worn Lace up boots for as long as I could remember. Momma liked the change in his appearance. He now looked like a gentleman rancher. All together I had dropped nearly two hundred dollars of my scholarship money. If I did not watch my money closer, I was going to have to go to work, and soon. I had no idea that college was so expensive.

I stopped by my apartment and picked up my dirty clothes and then headed East toward Tupelo. It seemed I had been away from home for a month, and it had only been three days. Classes would start on Monday, and I might be able to help out at the Law firm for a few hours or help Pappy on the farm. Willy had told me he was not able to leave until Friday, but he wanted to see if we could get Jessie and Penelope on a double date. The Idea sounded good. The girls were not taking summer school, so I was looking forward to seeing Penny again. I liked her a lot, but nowhere close to the way I had felt about Annabelle. She was fun to be with, but we had done no more than holding hands to this point. In many ways she reminded me of Anna. She was smart, beautiful, and witty, and she seemed to know her own mind. She loved her dad and was dedicated to seeing that he was well cared for, I didn't think that she would ever move out and leave him alone.

"AT THE ROOT OF JEALOUCY IS FEAR AND SADNESS."

Unknown Source

11

Ruffeled Feathers

WHEN I PULLED INTO the driveway an hour later Charlie and Billy Jackson were sitting on the front doorsteps. Charlie was ecstatic when she saw me. She was off the steps and flew into my arms as soon as I was out of the truck. Billy finally followed her over, the basketball under his right arm.

"Hey Billy, you still talking to my crazy sister? She's on parole, you know," I lied.

Billy laughed. He had caught on to the trick questions. "I don't think she is crazy though. Don't know what parole means. She's the smartest girl I know, and the prettiest too."

"Oh, what a sweet talker you are Billy," I said, letting Charlie slide from my arms. "She'll likely be asking you to marry her in a year or two. So, watch yourself."

"He's a lunatic Billy, and a gourd head to boot—pay him no attention."

"Billy, why don't you run on home for now, me and Charlie have to go in and see Momma and Pappy. You can come back tomorrow if you want. Maybe we can shoot some hoops."

Billy didn't look overjoyed about me sending him home, but he left, dribbling the basketball on the sidewalk.

"You want to kiss Bill goodbye?" I asked. "I'll turn my head."

Charlie was mad as a hornet at me now and ran ahead of me and went inside and locked the front door on me. Momma heard me yelling at her and came and opened the door.

"What a surprise. My son that doesn't care enough about his mother to give her a phone call."

I reached for her and pulled her near with one hand. I was still holding the bag of gifts in the other. She kissed me on the cheek and then swatted my backside.

"I ought to get a peach tree limb and wear it out on you."

"I'm sorry," I said, "I won't let it happen again. Where's Pappy and Robert Lewis?"

"Out back. Your daddy is helping Robert build a bird house for a project at school. I think they're through building, and Robert is painting. I will probably have to scrub him down with kerosene to get the paint off. Maybe your father too. I swear those two are like pigs in a sty when they start their building projects for school."

She had no sooner finished when the two misfits came through the back door. Robert had red paint from head to toes. Pappy wasn't much better.

"Painting bird houses, Momma says. What color?"

"Very funny," Pappy said. "Robert is a master Bird house builder, but not so good at painting. I'm done. Decided to come home early huh?"

"Yeah, Oxford is a graveyard, and the campus is not much better. I expect it will liven up some next week. They are expecting about three thousand students for summer school. I thought you might have a little work for me on the farm. Money don't go far at Ole Miss."

"As a matter of fact, I do have plenty for you to do. Me and Joe Webb bought the Taylor farm that Joins our place on the east. There are six hundred and forty acres of mostly pastureland. Fences are good, but a few spots need patching, and we need new gates to our place. Joe may want you to help him some, too. He took a hundred and forty acres, and I took the rest. Mr. Taylor passed away several months ago and his two daughters were married and away in Atlanta. They sold the farm at auction. We got it for thirty-five dollars an acre. We've got about a hundred acres suitable for corn or Soybeans. We'll plant it in corn most likely. I would like to rent it on the shares with someone."

"Willy will be here tomorrow late. He is short on cash too. We ought to be able to get up a couple of gates put up for you."

"I promised the kids you would take them to the picture show this weekend if you came home. Some show they want to see," Pappy said, shaking his head.

"*Paul Bunyan*" shouted Charlie. "The movie is about Paul Bunyan, Pappy."

"Don't think I ever heard of that feller," Pappy laughed.

"Well," I said, "I can't work on fences and take kids to the movie."

"Why don't you plan on working on the farm tomorrow and Friday and take the kids to the movie Saturday afternoon?" Pappy said. "Two bucks an hour for the hours you put in, and I foot the bill for the picture show."

"It's a deal," I said quickly. I didn't want him to change his mind. "But There might be four of us. Twenty dollars ought to cover it though."

Pappy cocked his head sideways and grimaced as if I had just crossed over his generosity line, but finally nodded his agreement.

"Who is the fourth person?" he asked.

"A friend of mine from school, Penny Johnson. That's a maybe though. I haven't asked her yet."

"You're taking a lot for granted. Loading her down with those two young ones. They can be a handful."

"The worst she can do is say no", I shrugged.

"She may never speak to you again," Pappy laughed.

"Guess you're right, but I like her a lot and I aim to ask."

Robert and Charlie were both listening with eyes wide until I mentioned Penelope. That is when Charlie stomped out of the room and went to her room and slammed the door.

"What's got into her?" Pappy asked. "Looks like you said something that got her feathers up."

"I have no Idea," I said. "I thought she would be tickled pink to get to go to the movies." Though I had a good Idea of what the problem was, but I didn't think it a good idea to tell Pappy.

"Must be a woman thing," Pappy added, "maybe Momma can talk with her."

"Good Idea," I said. I sure was not in a mood to try to settle her down. However, I should have known how she felt about me, and although she was only eleven years old, she was plain as day about her intentions toward me. Penelope was an obstacle to her plans, and that was scary. I felt like a brother to her, but she did not feel that way at all. A storm was brewing where she was concerned and sooner or later, I would have to face the issue.

I decided that I needed to go on with my plans to invite Penny, so I dialed her number while Charlie was still locked in her room.

"Hello," she answered.

"Hey," I said, this is Zack.

"Hey," she answered, "what's up? I was thinking about you, I was wondering if you would be home for the weekend."

"Well," I said nervously. "I was wondering if you would like to go to the movie Saturday Afternoon?"

"Sure" she answered, "What time?"

"2:00 Matinee. There's a catch though," I stammered.

"What's the catch?"

"I'm having to take my little brother and sister, Robert Lewis and Charlie. I don't think you have met them before."

"No but I've heard plenty about them from Annabelle. I'd like to meet them."

"There's another catch too. The movie is *"Paul Bunyan."*

"Sounds really romantic," Penny laughed. "Just my kind of movie. I'm all in if you promise to take me to see Cinderella later on."

"It's a deal. Now don't be surprised if Charlie is a little cold toward you, for she and Annabelle were really close, and she think's I shouldn't ever date again. Robert Lewis could care less, as long as he gets a milkshake and popcorn."

"Don't worry, Zack. I'm fairly good with kids, and I do plan on being a teacher."

"I'll pick you up about two o'clock Saturday afternoon," I said.

"Thanks for asking me, Zack."

"Thank you for agreeing to come on such short notice."

12

Building Fences

WILLY MADE IT HOME late Thursday. He wasn't happy about having to work Friday and Saturday, but when Pappy asked for help, we answered the call no matter what our plans were.

We drove up to the barn a little before six in the morning. The plan was to get an early start before it got to hot and take a long lunch break However the thermometer in the barn hallway read ninety- six. So much for a cool start.

"Lucas was already sharpening plow points by the red-hot forge when we stopped at the barn. Sweat rolled down his face and dripped off his chin. He took his red bandanna and wiped away the beads.

"Hot ain't it, Lukas?"

"If it ain't I've got a hell of a fever. Makes a man want to take up preaching. You boys better take plenty of water if you aim to do fencing. No shade out there where you're going to be working."

"Momma fixed us a gallon of iced tea. I think we'll be fine. By the way, how is the reading lessons coming?"

"Good. That Charlie is one smart little girl. She has got me reading the newspaper and I can write a little too. My spelling is not much, but she's determined that I'll be writing just about anything I want to by Christmas. I hope to be able to write my brother in Memphis; maybe

73

send him a Christmas card, if she doesn't give up on me as a hopeless case.

"Don't worry Lucas. Charlie will not give up on you. She may worry the stew out of you, but she will stick to it until you yell uncle."

"That time with Charlie on Sunday is the best part of my week. Sometimes Miss Owens comes with her and she's nice too. Never had two friends before. Sometimes the three of us take a walk so they can pet the new calves. Miss Owens loves to pet the cattle and they take to her like bees to honey."

"I'd like to take them to supper sometime but that will have to wait until I can save up enough to get me a truck."

"We drove to the place where we were to start. We could hear Lucas pounding on the anvil through the morning stillness. Lucas seemed like a man happy at his profession and was prideful in the work he produced."

We loaded 6x6 Posts to hang the gate on and 2x4's to cross brace just as Pappy has instructed. By ten o'clock we had set the gate post and braced each post as pappy had directed. We had just re-stretched the wire to the gate post when Pappy drove up with the ten-foot metal gate. Squat was riding shotgun, as usual, with his nose out the window. Pappy helped us hang the gate with squat watching from the shade of the truck. He pronounced it a job well done. He told us to climb in his truck and he would show us the new place he had purchased.

The new property was nearly all flat and level, except for a ridge that ran along the eastern side. A creek ran from the ridge down through the length of the sandy bottom. The creek was 30 yards wide in spots and appeared to be spring fed for the stream was clear enough to see the bottom in the shallow shoals.

Reckon there's any fish in that creek, Willy asked."

"I expect so, Pappy said. Joe claims he fished the stream until the old man died and then the kids had it posted. I aim to take the posted signs down, and I expect Joe will too."

Joe Webb rode up on his strawberry mare as we were hanging the gate.

"Mighty fine looking job you boys have done. Don't suppose I could hire you to build me one like it on my place?"

"I reckon so, I said. I sure could use the money.

I tell you what, I'll furnish the materials. You two do the work and I'll pay you fifty dollars."

Pappy spoke up. "Joe, you know you could get that job bone for half that much."

"Are you offering to do the job for half that AC?"

"Well no. You know I've got a bad back. Doctor Little says I don't need to be straining on it, Pappy grinned."

"Yeah, you probably paid him five dollars to say that. Me and Willy just grinned at the banter from two old friends."

"Didn't think so. You old tightwad." You probably have these boys working in this sun for half what it's worth.:

"Well, I have to feed them you know Pappy replied."

"Do you charge them board, too Joe asked with a sardonic grin.

"I ought to Pappy laughed. They eat like two brood sows that are about to deliver"

"Do we have a deal, boys?" Joe asked.

"Show us where you want the gate, and we start at 2 o'clock. Should be through by dark."

"We moved over to Joe's place, ate our sandwiches and drove over to the big pond and took a dip in the hottest part of the day.'

We finished the fencing job with time to spare even though the temperature was near a hundred degrees when we finished. We were home before five. Joe met us at the barn after we unloaded the tools. He met us as we were leaving and paid us in cash. Pappy paid us ten dollars each. It was a good day's work.:

We showered, changed clothes, and ate supper. Charlie was out of her room but was still giving me the stiff arm. I decided it was time to face the situation head on and went to the table where she was having milk and a peanut butter sandwich.

"Mind if I sit with you for a minute, Sis?"

"I'm not your Sis, and it's a free country. Sit where you want."

'I know that you are angry at me, but I don't know why. I can't fix the problem if I don't know what it is."

"Why did you invite that girl to go with us to the movies.

"That's it? You're angry because I asked Penny Johnson to go with us. "Listen now, Penny is my friend. Nothing more, Nothing less. "I am not in love with her, but I enjoy her company. I think you will too if you give her a chance. We are friends like you and Billy. I've known her from the time I met Annabelle. She and Anna and Jessie were like sisters. I know, for sure Anna would not want you to dislike or hurt Penny in any way. You enjoy spending time with Billy. He makes you happy. It is the same with Penny, and she is a friend I enjoy spending time with. I hope you will sleep on that and give Penny a chance at being your friend too."

Charlie was quiet but tears were forming in those beautiful blue eyes. I got up to leave. She looked up at me, her eyes now full of tears.

"Ok, she said through sobs, I'll think on it. And I'm not mad at you anymore."

"I went to her and hugged her and kissed her on her head. I was hoping I had mended my fences.

The phone rang just as I was leaving Charlie. It was Willy. He asked if I could meet him and Jessica at the Drugstore. I said sure, I would be there in about five minutes. I figured it had to do with another double date. I wanted to get to know Penny better, but I wanted to do it on my time schedule. They were seated in a booth near the back of the store where they filled prescriptions. Willy got up from sitting across from Jessica and sat down beside her. I sat across from them.

"What's cooking", I asked. You sounded as if it were urgent."

"Well, it is in a way. Jessie and I are driving over to Oxford tomorrow. She wants to see the campus. Thought you might want to ask Penelope to come along. We are going to drive by grandpa's place in Big Flat."

"that's a tempting offer, but I'll have to pass."

"Why?" Willy asked. What have you got to do that's so important?"

Promised to take the kids to the movie tomorrow afternoon. I've asked Penny to come too, and she accepted."

"Can't you worm out of it? Willy asked.

"Don't want to worm out of it Willy. A promise is a promise, and I intend to keep it. Pappy wouldn't take it lightly if I broke a promise to him. To say nothing of the kids. Sorry"

I got up to leave and it occurred to me that I had not talked to Marie Owens in two days. I went to the pay phone in the back corner and dialed her number.

"Hey, I said, what are you doing?"

"Drinking coco and watching the television."

"Where are you, Zack?"

"At the drugstore. I met Willie and Jessica for a few minutes, thought I would see if I could come by for a while.

"Sure, come on, I'll put on more coco, and we can talk. I've been missing you, wishing I could see you."

"I know, I have felt the same. I'll be there in two minutes."

I felt giddy as a schoolgirl when I parked in her drive. Marie met me at the door. This time she made no pretense, when I stepped through the door, she embraced me and kissed me full on the lips, and I returned the kiss. She was dressed in a Tee shirt and short Pajamas. She obviously wore no bra. Her body was warm against mine. 'She took her hand and guided it under the shirt to her breast. I massaged her nipples. She groaned. In seconds she had shed her shirt and she stepped out of her pajamas and stood before me naked except for her white panties, she took my hand and led me to her bedroom. She slid out of her panties and unbuckled my pants. I stepped out of them as they fell to the floor.

"Are you sure about this," I asked.

"No, I'm not, I only know that I want you to stay with me tonight. Make love to me, I don't want to be alone."

"We fell into her bed and let our hunger for each other have its way." We made love until we could do no more. She lay beside me, for a while, her head on my chest. Her long dark hair spread over my body. In minutes she moved upon me again and this time it was as if she were a part me, kissing and caressing, loving and exploring.

Minutes later she lay beside me, sleeping. Her sweet breath warning my chest."

"I don't know if Marie was in love with me, nor did I know if I loved Marie. It may have been that two broken people just needed someone to hold them in the darkness to ease the pain for just a while, and not feel the sorrow of being alone. When I got up to get dressed, she whispered to me.

"Stay the night with me Zack. I don't want to be alone tonight, and we can make love again when the sun comes up over the city."

I said, "Ok even though I knew that I shouldn't. Pappy would figure it out and so would Momma. But at the moment I didn't care. I only wanted to hold Marie Owens in the darkness."

When the morning came Marie came to me again, this time just to be held. She lay in my arms until the sun was rising above the Eastern hills. She then dressed and made coffee. We sat at the table. She offered to fix my breakfast, but I refused.

"Let's drive over and get breakfast and coffee. Will take only minutes, then I must go home. I promised to take the kids to the Movie at two this afternoon. There will be questions as to why I didn't come home last night. I don't like lying to my parents, but I don't think it would be a good Idea for either of us to tell them about our relationship."

"I agree she said. I know that we're consenting adults, because of my age some folks will think the worst of me. And maybe they should." Whatever you decide I'm with you."

"I wanted us to talk about the lawsuit that you're thinking of filing."

"Come by after the movie and I will fill you in on what I have learned, and you can tell me what my next step is to be.

"Yeah, I need to know what information you have, how did you come by it and what the plan is that you are considering."

"Good, she said, I am going to need you to help me with my plan."

"I'm going to pass on the breakfast, she added, you go on now and I'll see you after the movie."

"Ok, I said. I kissed her again and left her drinking her coffee."

I swung by the donut shop and picked up two dozen donuts, they were fresh out of the vat. I was hoping Charlie and Robert had not eaten. It was seven thirty when I pulled up in our drive. Momma and Pappy sat in the swing holding cups of coffee."

"What's in the boxes," Pappy asked.

"Donuts, I grinned, piping hot"

"Now you're talking, Pappy said. I do love donuts. Did you have to go to Birmingham to get them."

I got the dig. But said nothing. I

''Where's Willy, I asked after Momma had taken the two boxes of donuts and disappeared inside." Knew that sassing Pappy would be a losing proposition.

"Don't know where Willy is. Seems my sons no longer feel it necessary to let us know when they are going to stay out all night.

Yeah, I know I should have called, I stammered, but we were talking about law and time just got away from us. I should have been more considerate. For when I realized how late it was, I knew you and Momma would be upset."

"Well. Whatever you tell her, just do not try lying to her. She can read you like a cheap novel. She already has you pretty well figured out, but she will not ask you what you were really doing last night. I haven't told her anything, but it will not take two guesses for her to know the whole truth. You are eighteen now, and a grown man in many ways but grown men make stupid choices, and I figure you made one last night. I only hope it's not one that you will end up regretting the rest of your life."

Pappy had me nailed, and I knew it. It is strange how much clearer the picture is in the light of day. Strangely I felt no remorse or sorrow for what happened. It was over and done', and I figured it would not be the last time. I don't know if I was in love with Marie or not or if we were both just looking for a way to ease the pain of losing Annabelle. Whatever it turned out to be I wasn't going to regret the night I spent with her.

I sat at the table with Charlie, and we ate donuts and drank milk. Momma did not join us, but Pappy sat and drank his coffee and ate donuts and listened to Charlie and Robert chatter. Tomorrow Charlie would continue to be a teacher to Lucas and Pappy had promised he would take 'Robert fishing at the big pond while she was teaching. Robert loved fishing, and he and pappy were bantering back and forth about who was going to catch the most fish. We had all started to calling Robert just Rob. Except Charlie and Momma still called him Robert Lewis

Rob was growing fast and slimming down from that chubby five-year-old we had picked up at the Court House. He and Billy Jackson and Charlie played basketball almost every day until dark in the back yard. He had become quick and agile and showed promise of being a good athlete. Charlie couldn't stop talking about how much Lucas had learned since she had been teaching. He had learned to recognize many words and to write them. He had learned to add and subtract pretty good. She and Marie Owens had taught him how to fill out job tickets, which he was extremely proud of being able to do. Marie brought a small metal file cabinet for him to keep a record of the sales he made.

Charlie said she thought Lucas had a crush on Marie, but didn't think the feeling was mutual, but she did enjoy talking to him about his childhood and his blacksmith work. I finish eating and went to my room to get clothes together for the next week of school. It would probably be at least two weeks before I would be home again for, I would need to spend a lot of time in the books. I decided to pick up another class if my advisor would allow it Ole Miss had started allowing students to evaluate their skills in one hundred level courses. I decided to take the test for both English and Algebra one. I scored high enough to get credit for both classes and was given six credit hours. I had to scramble to pick up other courses but was able to pick up two classes in early American history.

The Jeffersonian Period and The Presidency of George Washington.

When two o' clock came the kids and I loaded into the truck and drove to Penny's house. She and a middle-aged man were sitting on the front steps. He wore an auto service uniform. I assumed it was her father. Penny wore jeans and a white blouse tied at the waist. She was beautiful. She motioned for me to get out of the truck and come to the porch. The three of us got out. Charlie ran to meet Penny. Charlie and Rob had surrounded Penny and she was introducing them to her dad.

When I got to the house, I shook hands with her father and told Him I was Zack Calloway.

"Frank Johnson," he said with a broad smile. "I have heard some about you Zack and saw your speech at graduation. Glad to meet you son. I would like to stop and talk to you and the young ones, but I've got work to do. If I get any more customers, I am going to have to hire some help. Good to meet you and the kids.".

There were cars and truck and trucks parked beside the shop, But the area was clean and orderly.

Penny ran to catch up to her father. When she yelled, he stopped and waited for her to catchup. She said something to him smiling that I couldn't hear. She gave him a hug and then turned and walked hurriedly back to the truck. We all piled in the truck and drove back toward town.

"Had to tell Pop that I had fixed his supper and it was all in the oven when he was ready. I usually cook him two meals a day—breakfast and supper.

"Don't your mother cook?" Charlie asked.

"Don't have a mother. Momma died when I was seven. She had cancer. "it's been just me and Pop ever since.

Charlie looked up at Penny with tears forming in her eyes. "Me and Robert lost our Momma too," I'm sorry you lost your Momma. I bet you miss her a lot don't you.?"

I sure do Charlie. But I'm thankful that I have Pop and good friends like Zack. I hope you and Robert will be my friends too. We kind of have something in common don't we."

"Charlie put her arms around Penny. "Can you come see me sometime Penny? Maybe we could take a walk around town or something. I don't really have a girl friend since Anna died. I know you were Anna's friend."

"I Would like that, but you would have to ask Mrs. Calloway, You could come to my house, and we could listen to music. Maybe even dance. Would you like that?"

"I sure would, I like Rock and Roll, do you?"

"Yep! My favorite. I've got lots of Elvis records, Buddy Holly, Fats Domino. Even Little Richard. And Jerry Lee Lewis. Anna and I and Jessica would listen to music for hours."

"I don't have any records, Charlie said but I listen to the Bandstand when I'm doing homework."

There was no doubt in my mind that Charlie and Penny were going to be ok. Rob didn't care what they did, he just wanted a basketball in his hands.

We made it to the theater in time to load up on soda pops and popcorn and were seated five rows from the front. I sat between Penny and Charlie. Rob sat by Charlie but halfway through he came to Penny and asked if he could sit with her. She gathered him into her arms and

81

in minutes he was asleep. I offered to take him off her hands, but she said no I've got it. After the movie I drove the kids home a little after four in the afternoon. Momma met Penny at the doorsteps and took Rob off her hands. I had made no other plans for the afternoon, but I enjoyed being with Penny and just took a chance and asked if she would like to go to the farm for a while and ride out to the new land that Pappy had purchased.

She said she would like to do that. We still had at least four hours of daylight and the temperature was not bad. Still in the high eighties, not bad for Hell and Mississippi.

Lucas was still working when we drove up to the barn. He stopped pounding on a wagon wheel and helped me saddle the horses. I saddled the black mare for Penny and Lucas saddled the steel gray for me. Penny wore no hat, so I got the Western Straw that I kept in the tack room. I also picked up two Cokes from Pappy's ice chest. The hat was a little large, but she looked great in it. We rode out past the big pond and out to where Willy and I had put up the new gate.

I dismounted and opened the gate and closed it when the horses were through. I led the way to the clear stream that ran through the acreage. The sun was getting low in the West, and we found a large willow that gave good shade and tied the horses and sat on the low bank along the edge of the creek.

"What did you think about the kids? I asked."

"Oh, they were great. I was surprised that they took to me so quickly" she said.

"Well, you are an easy person to like," I stammered like an oaf.

"Well thank you for that but do you know that I only had two dates all through High school. Both were with Naught McCullough. I liked him but not in a real romantic way. I do think he is a good person."

"Yeah, I think he is a good man and will make a great Marine."

"What about you, since Anna. Any romantic interests?"

"Well, I do have kind of a romantic interest", I said, looking sideways at her.

She smiled and said, "I'd be interested in why you would even like me. You are rich and handsome and really smart to boot. I am a daughter of an auto mechanic who I love more than life itself," she stated flatly. I doubt if Pop has more than a few hundred dollars in his bank account, there's a mortgage on our house and I own nothing of value."

First, I'm not rich, all I own is that old truck I drive. My father helps pay for my college, but he expects me to earn anything else I need. He believes that if a person doesn't earn what he has, he will not appreciate it. I have worked hard to keep my grades and have worked at the farm and at the law firm all through High School. I want to make my own way in the world not live on handouts from others. My Momma and daddy are wealthy. He has told me, and Willy will each get a portion of the farm when I finish school. I want to live out here. I love working on the farm."

I want to have a wife and children someday. I want them to be proud of me for what I've done, not what someone has given me. I want a wife who has her own mind and is not afraid to speak her mind to her husband. Rich or Poor does not matter to me as long as I have her whole heart."

Penny listened to me intently until I had finished. She moved over close to me she took off the hat and stood up."

"Stand up Zack."

I stood up and she hooked hands around my neck and pulled me to her. She kissed me and I returned it. She then lay her long blond hair against my chest and held me for a long moment.

She raised her head to me and said "Well?"

"Well, that's a dang good start," I stammered."

I kissed her again and then released her.

"It's time for me to go. She said, pushing me gently away. I told Pop I would be home early. He will worry if I'm late."

"Penny, I want to tell you that I will not be back from school for two weeks. I hope you will let me see you again. I want you to know too that I will be at Ole Miss for at least six years. If you do not want to get involved with a person who is going to be only an occasional date, I will understand six years is a long time for a girl to wait."

There is no such thing as a timeline for love, she said. If two people really love each other, they will find a way to make it work. I have promised Pop that I would wait till I finished college before I got serious with someone, and I intend to keep my promise to him. I think I will be able to finish my degree in three and a half years at the "W" and I hope I can find a teaching job here in Tupelo. I don't ever want to be too far from Pop", she said.

We rode up on the ridge and looked down on the creek and pasture below us. We found a spot surrounded by giant white oaks. "What a beautiful homesite this would be, "She exclaimed. It is so peaceful, and the view is lovely."

"Yes, I like it too. If Pappy gives me and Willy a choice, this is where I would pick to build a home."

We rode back to the barn and unsaddled the horses. Penny did not wait for help, she did it herself and carried the saddle to the tack room. Lucas had quit for the day, and he was walking from the big pond without a shirt. He had a towel across his shoulder. We waved to him as we were leaving. Ten minutes later. I turned into Penny's drive- way. She said she needed to go inside. She took my hand and patted it. "Call me when you leave for school., "oh yeah, I had a great time today.: She slid from the truck and waved goodnight. Halfway to the house she turned and waved again. I watched until she was inside. I really liked this girl and wondered if she would ever be a part of my life.

13

Meeting Gene Edwards

It was nearing seven o'clock when I finally made it to Marie Owen's place. There was a new Chevrolet parked in her Drive, and I was hesitant to call on her if she had visitors, but she was expecting me, so I went to the door. She answered the door in her usual attire, jeans and a Tee shirt. She smiled, and said "Come on in Zack, there's someone I want you to meet. When he stood up from the couch, I recognized the face, but couldn't recall his name. He offered his name and introduced himself.

"Gene Edwards," he said with a broad smile. "We have met before, but it has been a while back. You were Annabelle Owens boyfriend, I believe."

"That's right we had plans to be married right after high school, but as you know, those plans never worked out."

Marie could see that I was having difficulty making conversation and came to my rescue.

"Gene was appointed lead detective to investigate the wreck that killed Annabelle. He has given me information that I think might be helpful in the lawsuit that I plan to file. Why don't we sit at the table, and I'll make some coco and Gene can tell us what he knows about the wreck."

85

"To start off with, Zack, everything I tell you is public record—well almost everything. I discovered things that did not go into my report. Angela Winston, my assistant also helped to compile and record the report. She is a beautiful and very smart lady that can get information in a way that the person she is talking to doesn't even realize that they may be sending himself down the river. I mean she is a really good detective. To begin with, the Mississippi State Highway Police, impounded the vehicle as we do all vehicles where a fatality occurred, and towed it to our facility at Batesville. There it was gone over by our forensic and by our mechanical team from stem to stern. It is still in our custody, by the way. If you need to inspect the vehicle, let me know and I will go with you; otherwise, you will need permission from the state police."

"What we found I think your Lawyer friends will find very interesting. One thing they discovered was that the tie-rod on the left side was off its steering connector. The team was not able to determine if the tie-rod was off before or after the crash but considering the wear on the right-side tie-rod they thought this was the cause for the crash. I was sent to Memphis, to take a look at service records on the vehicle. Their office was located on highway 51 South, inside the Memphis city limits, they were not helpful and refused to show any records without a court order from a Tennessee judge, but the main terminal was across the state line with an address of Hernando, Mississippi. We were able to obtain service records for four years prior to the crash. We found that the company uses Statewide Truck Service for most of its mechanical repairs. The Owner of Statewide was very forthcoming about the work he has done for *Interstate Logistics*. That is the name of the trucking firm. We were able to make copies, of all records of work done for Interstate. You can look at all this information at our office in Tupelo as soon as we are finished. Once our report is complete, we will ship all records to Jackson."

"The rest of what I tell you is not on record. I'm by nature someone who tries to search for loose ends. One loose end is why there was no breathalyzer test given to the driver. The County sheriff was on the seen first, and then the Grenada police. The driver was taken by ambulance to the hospital in Grenada. It seems that the Grenada police assumed the Sheriff had performed the test, and the Sheriff deputies assumed that the Grenada police had performed the test. We are still waiting for the hospital to respond to our request to see if a test was performed by doctors there. I doubt if a test was performed there, because the driver was treated for minor injuries and then released. This is loose end that needs to be tied up, because if a test was not performed there's little chance criminal charges will be filed against the driver."

Marie brought coco and listened as Detective Edwards continued to lay out the investigation. I suddenly had a great deal of respect of the Mississippi Highway Police. "In addition, Angela, did a tour of bars in the area of the terminal. She found that the driver of the truck was a frequent customer at Tommy Johns bar and grill. Angela was with the FBI for six years before coming to work for us. She was tired of being sent to, God only knows where, every few months. Her specialty was tracking down offshore accounts of wealthy folks trying to avoid taxes. She is very good. Here she has a home and friends.

By cozying up to the owner who is the main bar tender, he disclosed that the driver had three shots of bourbon straight up. The day of the accident the bar tender also said he filled a half pint flask for the man before he left for the terminal."

My head was swimming after hearing the recap of what Edwards and his assistant had learned. I was anxious to talk to Mr. Webb about the case but would not get a chance to sit down with him for two weeks. I would give him a call however, as soon as I finished classes on Monday. How much of the information that the detectives had gathered could be used in court was for Mr. Webb to decide. But one thing was for sure, we had the makings of a huge case.

I got up to leave, and Edwards got up and shook my hand and wished me good luck at the University. And he added, "Thanks for looking out after Marie."

I got the feeling he knew more about our relationship than he let on. I wondered if Marie had talked to him about our relationship.

Marie walked me to the truck and told me to call her tomorrow night, that we needed to talk. I felt another storm brewing and was wondering where I would find shelter.

I drove home just as the rest of the family, including Willy were finishing supper. I suddenly realized I had eaten nothing but popcorn since breakfast. Momma set a plate in front of me, and I ate just about everything that was left.

Charlie wanted to know what Penny and I did after the movie.

"We went to the farm and rode the horses out to the new track of land that Pappy had purchased and sat by the creek and talked.

"My, my, what an exciting date you are. Didn't even buy her dinner? That's probably the last you'll see of her. If she's smart, she will mark you off of her list of possibilities."

"You're being mean, and Pappy needs to turn you across his knees and give you a good swatting."

"It's not me that needs the swatting, gourd head. It's you," Charlie retorted.

"Charlie is right only I need to use a ball bat to your noggin", Pappy laughed.

I finished eating, gathered the clothes I would need for the next week and headed for the door. Charlie and Rob came to give me a hug, and Momma brought me a jar of blackberry Jelly she had canned. She, as always, gave me a hug and kiss and told me to behave myself. I took the highway west toward Oxford. I turned the radio on a Memphis station and listened to Little Richard wailing "Lucille." There was not much traffic for a Sunday night, and I pulled up to my apartment in just about an hour. Tomorrow I would start classes but tonight I doubted if sleep would come easy.

14

Becoming A Military Man

CLASSES ON MONDAY WERE, for the most part, just an explanation of what the teacher expected, and how they would grade. They lasted no more than thirty minutes. We would get down to business at the next meeting.

I had decided to take Willy's advice and file paperwork to join the AFROTC. He would let me know the next day if the directors had approved my application. We would have morning drills each day for thirty minutes before classes started. I would receive four hours credit in addition to the classes in Military History. This was one night a week, if the numbers worked out.

I soon got into the routine and enjoyed the classes in Military science. Willy was instructor in Military basics, Line of command, Ranks, and basic drill techniques. He was much better at it than I expected, and he seemed to enjoy ordering me around. The one thing I had not counted on was one summer I would have to go on active duty for six weeks. If I completed the courses successfully, I would be a Second Lieutenant in the U.S. Air Force as soon as I earned my degree.

Since I would be heading to law school after undergraduate school, I would most likely serve as an assistant in the Legal department.

I called and was able to talk to Mr. Webb at the law firm for a few minutes on Monday and explained what I knew about the case. He said it would be a costly venture for the firm but could also be a big return if we should win the case. He wanted to talk with Marie, but I was doubtful if she would talk with him unless I could accompany her, and I did not intend to be back in Tupelo for two weeks. He said that was fine, that he would make time for her even if was after hours.

I called Marie and told her that Mr. Webb was interested in the case and wanted to sit down and talk when I got home in two weeks. She agreed. She also told me of developments at her work. The bank was going national and wanted her to take a temporary assignment in Seattle where they had purchased three well established family-owned banks. She would oversee all the accounting functions and would get a hefty salary to boot.

How long is the assignment for? I asked.

A year, maybe longer. It may be permanent. It will be my choice.

I almost swallowed my tongue. I couldn't believe what I was hearing.

"How on earth can you just up and leave. I thought I meant more to you than that."

"That's why I'm going to take the transfer. The thing between us would never work, and I think you know that. This will give us both time to let our emotions cool and perhaps find someone our own age. I know you have been seeing Penelope Johnson. She is a sweet girl and maybe it will give your relationship time to develop. I will stay until I have finished the courses that I am taking at the extension. That will be about a month. I also intend to take my CPA exam before I leave, but I can do that any time.

I was dumbfounded. How did she know about Penelope? Who could have told her? Was that the real reason she was leaving?"

I did not know what to say, for I knew she was right about us. As much as I cared for her, trying to explain it to my family would be dang near impossible. Momma might just shoot me.

"What am I going to tell Charlie? I asked. She loves you dearly."

"Nothing, she said. I will tell her. I want to be the one to explain. If she is angry, I want her to be angry with me and not you. You are the light in her life. She loves you."

"So, I'm not going to see you for a year? I said. I'm not sure I can handle that."

"It is the best for both of us, but I want you to know that I will always love you. I think you saved my life. I am not sure that, without your support, I could have survived the loss of Annabelle."

"I have to go now, but I will see you in two weeks."

I hung up the phone, but I felt sick. For the first time I realized just how much I cared for Marie Owens.

Two weeks later

I picked up Marie at her house just after five for our appointment with Mr. Webb at his law firm. The firm was closed for the day, but, as usual his secretary was still working. She showed us into Mr. Webb's small conference room. She seated us and said that she would get Mr. Webb and would be right back.

Mr. Webb came in seconds later. He had shed his jacket and wore a white shirt and tie. He looked like he had just opened for the day. I stood up and made the introductions, for Mr. Webb had not met Marie Owens. Shortly after we were seated Mr. Webb's secretary, Mrs. Free came in carrying a fresh legal pad and a small portable tape recorder. Mr. Webb introduced Mrs. Free to Marie and started the meeting by assuring Marie that everything that she told us would be kept strictly confidential.

I asked Marie to tell Mr. Webb everything that she knew. She said she would but would not reveal any names of the persons who had given the information until he had determined if he would take the case.

"The people who have given me this information, she began, are highly respected, professionals and I do not want to do anything that might tarnish their reputation or cost them their jobs."

"Although the information I am giving you will soon be available for the public to read. The less we can keep them out of the case, the better it will be."

Marie removed sheets of paper from her purse and began to tell all that the Highway Police had learned. She also told us me that there would be more information coming, for his assistant was digging into the possibility that the owner of the trucking firm might have offshore bank accounts where he was hiding money from Federal and state officials. This, in my view made this a dangerous case.

"When she had finished, she told us that she had developed a new accounting system for the banks where invoices and any expenditures or revenue would be accounted for by numbers instead of the old way of all entries on the same ledger. The system is not really all that new, she said, but the system for coding entries is my own, and it allows for multiple accounts to be managed under one single bank account. It can drastically cut the number of employees required in the accounting department of any large business. I want to use this to try to sell it to the trucking firm to gain access to their files in Tennessee.

"And if this plan doesn't work?" Mr. Webb asked.

"Then we have to go with what we have, Marie answered, but don't sell me short. I can be very persuasive," as she gave a devilish grin to Mr. Webb and that thing that all women do with their eyes, which drive men nuts.

"That brought a smile and a little squirm from Mr. Webb and a laugh from Mrs. Free.

"This kind of case can take a considerable amount of resources which my firm may not have. We will for sure have to hire extra office staff and a top-notch detective. The payoff could be huge if we win and nothing if we lose."

"I have a hundred thousand, Marie offered."

That startled me. I looked at Marie with raised eyebrows.

"You have a hundred thousand dollars?"

"Yes, from a life insurance settlement. I'm willing to risk it all if we need it."

"Well, that puts a little different light on the project."

"We would normally get a thirty Percent part of any settlement, but if you put up this money, we will reduce our fee to twenty five percent and will only draw on your money in case of an emergency, which I don't think will be necessary. We are a small firm but have substantial reserves."

"Marie said she would put up the money as soon as we file suit."

"Mr. Webb agreed that we would take the case but wanted to have plenty of time to do his own investigating. And time to decide how much he would ask for in the suit. It would be in the millions but not so much to cause them to file for bankruptcy. He said we would talk again in December when things were usually slow at the law firm, and we would decide when the appropriate time was to bring the suit.

Three weeks passed before I talked to Marie again. She called to tell me she had taken the CPA exam and felt good about her prospects of passing the whole three- part exam in the first sitting. I wished her the best and told her I would be home in a week. It would be the end of the first summer session. I asked if I could come by but; she hesitated a few seconds and then said no, it would be best if I didn't. She promised she would call in a week, when she was to get the results of her tests.

I hung up the phone, once again feeling the same emptiness that I had felt when I lost Annabelle.

I had a lot of reading to do for finals and lay across my bed and began reading Thomas Paine's *"Common Sense."*

I finished my finals the last week in June and went home for the weekend and would not return to classes until the fifth of July. Professors posted grades on their office doors the day after the tests, and I checked each class before I left. I had managed A's in all classes—even in my Military science class. Marie called as I was packing my clothes for the weekend, to tell me she had passed her CPA and would soon be implementing her plan to gain access to the trucking firm files. I told her to be careful.

"Of course," she said, and hung up the phone."

I had called Penny nearly every night just to talk. I really liked her a lot but was not sure where our relationship was going. We had not been on a real date, and I was not sure I could handle another disappointment in a love relationship. I would ask her out the next time I was home though. She was really a nice girl, and I did not want to toy with her emotions. I had little time to spend in a relationship and Penny deserved much more.

I drove by the AFROTC building to see if Willy was going to make it home for the fourth of July Holiday.

93

"No, he said, I have work to do, and Jessie is driving over here tomorrow. We are going to do a picnic in the Grove and then watch fireworks. Have to oversee presentation of the Flag and Taps for the veterans. Say hello for me. I know mom and dad will be disappointed that I will not be home."

15

Makings Plans for Lawsuit

I MET WITH MR. Webb in his conference room the day before my nineteenth birthday. Mrs. Free had set up the speaker phone where we could talk to Marie, and she could hear each of us. This was new technology to me, and I was impressed at how well it worked. Mr. Webb had two issues he wanted to resolve. First, was when we needed to file suit, and secondly, how much money we were going to sue for.

It was agreed that we would file suit in Circuit Court, in Grenada four weeks prior to the expiration date which would be in November 1961. The amount of the suit would be for twenty-five million. We knew that the trucking firm had assets in the hundreds of Millions. The company owned terminals in forty-five states and a massive truck fleet. It was decided that we would ask an additional ten million in punitive damages. We would hope for a sizeable settlement without a jury trial, but we had to be prepared for a lengthy trial.

Before we ended the call, I finally had a chance to ask Marie how the new job was going and how she liked the Northwest.

"The job is great, but the weather is awful. I found a small cottage in the suburbs and take the bus to work. Don't know if I'll ever drive in this city. Traffic is awful too."

I said goodbye and Marie was gone once again, and I was sick to my stomach. I wanted to see her."

I celebrated my nineteenth birthday at home with the family, Charlie was ecstatic that I was going to be home for a week. She had turned twelve and had grown a good two inches. She was filling out all over and I noticed she was now wearing a bra. I guess that is a sign a girl is easing into womanhood. A day I figure that they will curse the rest of their lives.

"Charlie was going to be a beautiful woman If her present state was any indication of her future looks. Billy Johnson was still a daily fixture at our house, but when I was home Momma said he wouldn't come over. She wanted to know if I had scolded him.

"Of course not, I like Billy even if he is a pest sometimes."

Pappy was still spending most of his days at the farm. Up to three hundred head of Herford's he said, and it has been a job keeping hay out during the winter. I've hired Notch McCullough to help feed after school. He is mighty good help, and I let him drive the old truck some. He'll be a Junior in high school next year, and says he is going to follow his brother into the Marines. He has promised he will finish school though. He is a heck of a football player they say, and I aim to go watch him some next year. Joe Webb uses him some on his place too. They seem to get on very well. I think Joe is sweet on his mother.

I called Penny to see if she wanted to take in a movie, but she said no but asked me to come over to her place for a while. We could just talk for a while. I have learned that when a woman says she wants to talk, there is something serious on her mind, and it's usually not a positive development. At any rate, I told her I would be over about seven.

Penny was waiting for me on the porch steps when I drove up. She stood up and dusted the seat of her jeans and met me as I stepped from the truck. She surprised me with a hug and a kiss on the cheek.

"Wish I had come sooner," I said, as she took my arm and led me to the house. What's up? I asked. Never knew you to turn down a movie date.

"It's Pop. He sprained his back today and I didn't want to leave him. He says he is going to be ok, but he can hardly stand. He closed the shop until Tuesday. I'm trying to make him rest. Thought we could play records or sit on the porch and talk. I want to know how school is going and what you have been up to. It seems like forever since I have seen you.

"Yeah, I know. Telephone conversations are not like being here with you."

I filled her in on my signing up for AFROTC and that I was a student under my brother. We made small talk about the near future, and I told her I was getting a chance to work on a really big legal case with Mr. Webb. I told her I couldn't talk about it, but it is a great learning experience. I told her I would be here for the new years and the week following but would probably not be back home again for a while.

"Perhaps you could come to Oxford one weekend, I said. I could show you around the campus and my apartment."

She cocked her head sideways, her palm on her chin and her arm resting on her knee and smiled.

"Maybe she said, but it would just be for the day. That has to be understood."

"Ok. I respect your stance on the issue."

She had subtly but firmly established the limits of our relationship, and I was ok with that.

We talked for nearly three hours before I told her I best go. I asked if she wanted to go to the football field tomorrow night to watch fireworks with the family.

"I'll have to let you know. Depends on Pop's condition. I will call you after noon tomorrow.

She called and told me her dad was hardly able to stand but refuses to see a doctor. "Perhaps you could come over and visit for a while Monday, before you leave for school."

I said I would be sure to do that, and she promised to make me lunch.

"Sounds great, I said, and you have surprised me once again. I didn't know you were a cook."

"Well, I wouldn't exactly say I'm a cook. I just barely can make do, thanks to my mother. I'm doing spaghetti for dinner. Hope it's eatable."

"That's my favorite."

"THERE ARE FOUR BASIC HUMAN NEEDS,
FOOD, SLEEP, SEX, AND REVENGE"

Balnksy

16

Marie Works Her Plan

THE WEATHER WAS SCORCHING hot and steaming when she parked her leased, sky-blue, Ford Thunderbird in the visitors parking area of Smithfield Logistic and Transportation Company.

The building was a four stories steel and brick structure that filled a city block on Highway 51 South, a mile from the Mississippi State Line.

Marie Wore a black, knee length skirt that showed off her shapely legs. She wore a white silk blouse unbuttoned just to show a hint of cleavage. She wore three-inch stiletto heels that she had practiced for a week walking on so she could show off the maximum of her sexy body. Her long blond hair, that she had paid fifty dollars to get dyed, fell in ringlets around her beautiful face, and a colorful scarf that she draped over her shoulders and tied in a knot around her neck. She had paid another two hundred dollars for the newest thing in blue contact lenses to cover her black eyes. She wore enough make-up to bring cover to any lines around her eyes. She was a beautiful and sexy woman. She was on a woman on a mission.

Marie had a fashionable bag draped across her shoulders.

She walked through double glass doors to a broad atrium where four guards monitored television screens that scanned the floors and hallways. She walked up to the Guard that appeared to be the person in charge. She pulled a business card from her bag and handed it to the guard. He looked her up and down.

"I was wondering if I might be able to see Mister Smithfield. We have a mutual friend and she asked me to stop by if I was in the neighborhood."

He looked her up and down again and at the business card again. "Hold on a sec he said turning around in his chair and picking up a red phone, directly behind him. He spoke a few words into the phone and then turned back to Marie.

"He said you could have ten minutes, if you follow me, I will take you to his office."

Smithfield's office was on the second floor, a space where other executives were located. She was led to a large office just steps from the elevator. The door was opened so Smithfield motioned them in with eyebrows raised.

Marie reached out her hand and introduced herself.

"I am Marie Thompson, CPA, she said as he took her hand. I believe we have a mutual friend, in Miss Angela Winston.

"Yes, Winston, he said, is a beautiful woman. We've had a drink together a few times. She is in insurance, I believe.

"I'm not sure what her business is, Marie said, we have a group of single women who get together once or twice a month and have dinner and a glass of wine. She is a fun-loving young woman and a close friend. She helps me out from time to time when I'm in a bind."

Smithfield offered her a chair and she sat in a padded chair in front of his desk. Smithfield moved out from behind his desk and sat down directly across from her.

"I will not waste your time Mr. Smithfield; I own a small accounting firm in Tupelo and have developed a new coding system for companies who have a large accounting department and would like to cut their expenses by at least forty percent and have a system that gives you really fast access to all your accounting information. I was hoping we could perhaps have a drink, or possibly dinner and let me explain my system. The cost to you would be very modest and would be recouped within months. I have already put the system in place at one of Tupelo's largest banks. It is working well, and it saves the bank more than three thousand dollars per month. "Do you like to dance, Mr. Smithfield?"

"I do like to dance and would like to have dinner with you. When would you be able to do that?"

"Well, I have clients in Memphis that I am to call on this afternoon. But I should be finished by four. Are you familiar with Jimmy John's Bar and Grill?" They have a cozy little place with a nice dance floor and a live band.

"Yeah, I go there sometimes, he said, and the food is great too. Shall we meet at five."

"That sounds good, she smiled.

"She got up to leave and handed him a business card. Marie had the telephone company install an answering Machine when she was away. If Smithfield called, he would get her answering system, telling him to leave a message. He slipped the card in his shirt pocket. Marie walked toward the door. He watched her every move until she reached the door.

"Wait," he said, I will walk you out, lest the guards harass you."

Smithfield followed Marie outside to her car. She made sure that he got a good look at her legs as she slid into the Thunderbird and started the engine.

"See you at Jimmy John's at five as she waved goodbye and roared away."

"My, My, he muttered. Now there is a woman. A real woman he said, shaking his head. I don't care what she is selling. I'm buying."

"Marie was not a drinker, but she had been drinking wine lately, just practicing seeing how much she could tolerate and keep her senses. She had never led a man on before, but this was business and she had to play it smart.

Mike Smithfield was waiting with a corner table when Marie arrived a little after five.

"I'm sorry, she apologized, I signed two new companies today and just finished touring the accounting departments. I see you have already ordered a drink."

"Yeah, what will you have? He asked, waving a hand for the waitress.

"Red wine for me. she said, and I need it. It's been a very long day, and I have to drive back to Tupelo tonight. I have an important client to see at eight in the morning. It's a small law firm but has a sizeable accounting department."

"While we are waiting for the drinks, why don't I tell you a bit about what I do and if you're interested, I will come by and review your accounts with your accounts supervisor and give you a sample of what we can do. I will need access to all revenue and expenditures as well as personnel files for at least one quarter of your financial year. It will take me two days at the most. I will then provide you with a printout you can give to your board of trustees. To explain how the new system works. Perhaps I could come to your board meeting.

She put her hand on his arm as she spoke, and he placed his hand on top of hers.

The waitress brought their drinks, and she took two or three sips and asked him if he would like to dance. The live band had not arrived and the Disc Jockey was playing an Elvis Song that was slow enough to waltz to. She took his hand and led him to the dance floor. It was obvious that he couldn't wait to get her in his arms. She held him far enough at bay to keep him interested, but not so close he could feel all the merchandise. When the dance was over, they sat at the table and finished their drinks and ordered sandwiches.

"Best French dip sandwiches in all of Memphis, he said. I eat here a lot."

She ate half of a huge sandwich with chips which was delicious.

Oh my," she said rolling her eyes, this is so good. We have to do this when I have time to stay over, and we can visit."

"When will you have time to review our files, Smithfield, asked. Soon I hope."

'Well, this week is filled, but Monday or Tuesday I could come and start the review process. I will bring my assistant on Tuesday if there are a lot of files. He is a student at Ole Miss and a good friend of my daughter. He is very fast and thorough and needs to work. We will need two, maybe three days to enter the information converted to our system. I think your board will be amazed at how efficient the system is. Your initial investment will be in equipment. Three typewriter type machines that reads a perforated tape.

Our system requires this special kind of machine that we enter our new codes into, and the machine will print out the report." The machines will replace at least two people, which saves the company salaries and whatever you pay out in benefits. The machines run about a thousand dollars. My fee is twenty-six hundred for our services for one year. This is to give you time to train your employees. We will be at your disposal to answer any questions you may have. We will require no money on our part until the system is operational."

Smithfield was hooked, now all Marie had to do was to reel him in, to open all his files to her. Marie took another sip of her drink, patted Smithfield on his hand as she stood.

"I'm sorry Mike, I hate to leave such charming company, but I have to drive back to Tupelo tonight, and I don't want to get stopped for driving under the influence of Mike Smithfield.

Smithfield started to stand and protest, but she reached over and pecked him on the cheek and whispered "I'll see you next week. Don't drink too much. She worked her way across the crowded dance floor and out the door. Two hours later she was at her home in Tupelo. She called Zack at a little after nine. She related to him the events of the day and told him she would need him in Memphis on Tuesday, and it would be helpful if he could meet with her Monday night to finalize her plans. Angela Winston had given her the name of the driver of the big rig. His name was Ben Adams. She also had his address and telephone. His home address was given as Hernando Mississippi. That was a stroke of luck, she could start to review the files beginning with A thru B and if he was still employed, there should be a record of any traffic violations including accidents that he was involved in. Zack agreed and said he would meet her Monday night at seven.

"EVERYBODY HAS A PRICE; THE IMPORTANT THING IS TO FIND OUT WHAT IT IS"

Pablo Escobar

17

Zack Assists Marie

ZACK EXPLAINED TO WILLY that he needed to be excused from drills on Tuesday morning but would be back on Wednesday. Marie had enlisted the help of Angela Winston to review all the files and help enter the information they gathered into the machine. Smithfield had set aside a conference room with a board-room size table where Marie could set up her machines and a copy Equipment, and plenty of room to review files. The new process was a little cumbersome, but it did not take long for Angela to get the hang of what she was doing, and the process moved quickly. Angela made notes of every unusual expenditure or revenue and within hours she knew that Smithfield was hiding money in offshore accounts. Marie had accomplished in one day, what she had worked for months on. When the first quarter of expenditures was complete the personnel files were reviewed, and Zack had run the information through the new machine, he had a complete printout of all employee activity for the first quarter to present to the board. While Zack managed the mechanics, Angela was busy gathering information on the company's many bank accounts. It was plain that the company was hiding millions in offshore accounts, and she was soon able to identify where the money was going and how they were hiding it.

Marie was introduced to the board by Mike Smithfield on Thursday evening at seven o'clock. Marie introduced Zack as her technical assistant. Angela did not attend the meeting lest Smithfield became suspicious. Marie had made packets explaining her program to hand to each board member. She had spent almost two hundred dollars to have the packets oriented in color and on heavy, slick bond paper. It was a very professional job. She went through the packet with all board members allowing time for questions. Only a few were interested enough to ask intelligent questions. She then asked Zack to feed the tape through the machine. The Machine ran the tape at over a hundred-fifty words per minute. The members were in awe when the first quarter of revenue and expenditures were printed out in a little over ten minutes. When Marie had finished with revenue and expenditures Marie pointed out that the number of trucks and the number of drivers did not equate. That the company was paying for over two hundred and ten drivers when there were only a hundred and ninety trucks in their fleet. This brought Smithfield to his feet.

"Thank you for your presentation," he said. "I will discuss your program with the board and the cost to our company. The program is very impressive. Thank you too for pointing out the discrepancy in our ratio of drivers to the size of our fleet. We will look into the matter with our accounting director."

Smithfield called for a ten-minute break, to say goodbye to Marie, and allow Zack time to clear his equipment from the room. Board members were eager to get a closer look at this beautiful woman. A half hour later, Zack had packed the machine and the tapes in his truck and headed for Oxford. Marie was on her way to Tupelo. Smithfield did not know it at the time, but it would be nearly three years before he saw Marie Owens or Zack Calloway again. Marie had finished what she set out to do. She and Angela Winston had gathered a ton of information. It would now be up to Justin T Webb to find Justice for her and her daughter.

Just before noon Saturday morning Marie boarded a Delta Airlines plane out of Memphis for a seven-hour flight to Seattle Washington. She would keep her home in Tupelo, but she doubted that she would ever return to Anna's town. She loved Zack Calloway, but she was determined to make a new life for herself and let Zack pursue his dreams with a younger woman. She was certain that he was going to make a fine Attorney and he would make someone a fine husband. She lay her head back and closed her eyes. Sleep, however, would not come. Her mind was on the events of the past few days and how easily she had deceived Mike Smithfield. She didn't feel good about that, but she and Angela Winston had uncovered enough information to help Mr. Webb in her lawsuit and she was sure when the civil suit was settled, the FBI would want some of Smithfield too. She would like to see Smithfield's face when he tried to locate her and learned that Marie Thompson didn't exist. He would also try to find Marie Thompson, CPA. He would also learn that there was no such business located in the city of Tupelo.

She would call to tell him that the Justo Writer company, which made the machines that she used, were on strike and that it might be months before they would be able to deliver his equipment. She hoped that he would not figure it all out before Mr. Webb filed her Lawsuit.

*"ANY LAWYER WORTH HIS SALT KNEW THE
FIRST OFFER SHOULD BE REJECTED"*

John Grisham

18

Lawsuit is Filed

JUSTIN WEBB FILED THE lawsuit on November 30th, 1961, with the Circuit Court's office located on the second floor of the Grenada County Courthouse, Grenada, Mississippi. He hand delivered the filings, not wanting to take a chance with the Postal Service. The Suit, "Marie Ann Owens vs Smithfield Transportation and Logistics Company, AKA Smithfield Transport. Was front page news in the Clarion Newspaper in Jackson and Newspapers in Tupelo and Memphis. The Webb law firm was awash in phone calls from across the country seeking more information on the case. "No Comment," was the only answer they got.

The suit asked for damages in the amount of twenty-five million dollars, and punitive damages in the amount of five million. The suit alleged that Smithfield Transportation was negligent in the maintenance of their vehicle that killed her daughter, Annabelle Owens, in January of 1958. It was also negligent in the hiring of the driver of the truck involved in the accident, when the records showed the driver had a history of alcohol abuse and had been cited on numerous occasions for reckless driving, and failure to maintain control of the vehicle in which he was driving.

I called the number Marie had given me to call in Seattle if I needed to talk to her, but only got an answering machine. The time had now come for Marie to try to get justice for her daughter. I had waited for this day too. I only hoped that the small firm of Justin Webb was able to handle a whole gaggle of lawyers that a company like Smithfield was capable of throwing at him. He had hired additional staff and cajoled his nephew, who had established a small private law firm in Memphis to give him a hand with the legal issues. There was nothing I could do but listen and learn.

I finished my undergraduate degree at the end of December. I had already registered for classes in the law school in the middle of January. The course offerings for Spring Semester were Limited but was able to get enough courses to keep me busy. By the last of May I had completed one semester at the Ole Miss Law school. It was a grueling Grind of endless research and opinions, readings and writing. There were, however, bull sessions with fellow students that I enjoyed and was quite a learning experience.

Judge Horace McFadden, set the trial date to begin March 2, 1962. The small courtroom was filled to capacity and there were dozens of news persons and curiosity seekers outside the courtroom to try to get news of what was going on inside. I had made arrangements with all my professors to attend the first day of the trial. Mr. Webb allowed me to sit at his table with his nephew and his secretary Mrs. Free.

'At eight O'clock the Circuit clerk asked the court to rise as the judge entered the courtroom. The judge gave a few instructions and then asked that jury selection begin. The first few hours were dedicated to this process. The Jury of six men and five women was finally selected by three o'clock in the afternoon and Judge McFadden recessed the court shortly after giving the jury instructions, until eight the next day.

Day two of the trial, both sides in the case were allowed twenty minutes for each side to give opening statement. Mr. Webb wore a dark three-piece suit and starched white shirt and a red and blue striped tie which were traditional Ole Miss colors. He began his usual ritual of removing his jacket and loosening his tie, before walking over to face the Jurors. His deep baritone voice echoed through the courtroom when he began his opening statement. "Ladies and Gentlemen, of the Jury. Miss Anabelle Owens was killed on highway 51 South of

Grenada, just a few miles from here, nearly three years ago, when the driver of a Smithfield Trucking eighteen-wheeler lost control of his vehicle and crashed into a vehicle headed North. Three people were killed in the accident.

We will show that Smithfield Trucking was negligent in its failure to keep its vehicle in good repair, and we will also show it was negligent in its hiring drivers for its business. Jury members please pay close attention for ten minutes, to the facts in this case as we present them. My client Mrs. Marie Ann Owens seeks justice for her daughter Annabelle, who was coming home from a visit to the University of Mississippi School of medicine, in Jackson, where she had been accepted and was to begin her lifelong dream of becoming a doctor in the fall of that year. Mr. Web slapped his hand on the rail of the jury box and thanked the jury for their service to the community and moved back to take his seat. His opening statement had taken less than six minutes.

Brevity was not to be the case with the Smithfield attorney. He contradicted everything the Mr. Web had said and blamed Annabelle for her own death. Which brought groans from the audience, and a warning to the audience. He droned on about how much Smithfield Trucking meant to Mississippi and its excellent safety record. He said such a settlement would likely bankrupt the company, causing the loss of hundreds of jobs to the state and the country. If you listen to the facts in this case, as Mr. Webb has said, you will find in favor of Smithfield trucking.

When the opening statements were over. Judge McFadden instructed Mr. Webb to call his first witness

I call Mr. Mike Smithfield. A mummer went through the audience. I was also wondering why he called Mr. Smithfield so early in the trial.

Mike Smithfield had been in court many times and was not intimidated by any lawyer. He was dressed sharply in a three-piece expensive Lenin suit and looked very confident in the Witness Chair.

Mr. Smithfield you hold the title of President and CEO of Smithfield. Is that Correct?

"Yes, I am CEO, President, and Complete owner of the truckline."

"In other words, you answer to no one where your trucking firm is concerned. Is that right?"

"Yes. that is true, but of course I answer to my customers."

111

"Mr. Smithfield, your company is licensed to do business in Mississippi. But your home Office is located in Tennessee. Your Mailing address is Highway 51 South, Hernando, Mississippi. Is that correct?"

"Yes, it is correct, a currier delivers our mail each day."

"Mister Smithfield, I have a copy of a form here from the secretary of State's office in Jackson, that you are required to file each year. Would you take a look at the form and tell me if that's your signature at the bottom of the form?

"Yes, that looks like my signature."

"On this form you have listed all bank accounts, and the average daily balance for each one. You also list the assets and liabilities of your business which are located in other states. The State of Mississippi does not require you to list your assets and bank accounts in other states. Why did you do that?

"Just a matter of complete disclosure," Smithfield Answered.

"I see, Mr. Webb nodded.

Mr. Smithfield just as a matter of full disclosure the statement shows your assets as being over 600 million dollars and your liabilities as being less than half that amount. Is that correct?"

"Well, that amount varies throughout the year, but yes that's correct for the day the disclosure was signed."

"One last question, Mr. Smithfield. Do you have any other accounts that are not listed on this ledger?

"Objection, your honor where is going?"

"Overruled. The witness will answer. You opened this can in your opening statement Mr. Barnett."

"No, there are no other accounts or assets."

Mr. Webb countered. "Let me remind the witness that perjury is a crime. Would you like to change your answer sir?"

"NO!" the witness shouted. He was red faced and obviously very upset.

Mr. Webb entered the form into evidence and excused the witness. The defense chose not to cross.

Judge McFadden called an hour and a half for lunch and the whole courtroom headed for the door. The defense had their heads together in obvious turmoil. Mike Smithfield already had it figured and wanted to talk. Jack Burnett motioned for Mr. Webb for a conference. The Circuit Clerk showed them to a conference room just off the Judges chamber.

Mr. Webb called me aside and said it's early in the trial to be talking settlement, but you best have Marie waiting by the telephone just in case.

I called Marie's number from a pay phone on the ground floor of the Courthouse, and as usual got her answering machine. I left a message for her to stay by her phone. I told her I would call in the evening to keep her informed. I returned to the conference room where Mr. Webb his secretary, and his nephew were seated at a conference table across from Mr. Smithfield and his lead attorney, Mr. Edwin Barnett.

Mr. Webb opened the discussion. "You asked me here for a purpose Mr. Barnett. What do you want to talk about?"

"Mr. Webb. You know that Jury is not going to award you such a large amount. Let's try to agree on a reasonable figure and we can all get on to other important matters.

"I believe Mrs. Owens would entertain a reasonable offer, but I need to hear an amount."

"Mr. Smithfield is willing to offer five million."

"I thought you said reasonable offer, Mr. Barnett."

"It's doubtful if Mrs. Owens will even entertain such a token amount, but I will call and ask." Mr. Webb picked up the phone in the conference room and dialed the number. Mr. Webb talked on a phone provided by the Circuit Clerk's office. He had his back to those in the room as he spoke only a few words and then hung up the phone and took his seat at the table.

"My client said that five million is not going to buy you a settlement. Her counter is twenty-five million and we forget the five million in punitive damages.

"That's ridiculous. This meeting is over."

"Don't be so impulsive Mr. Barnett. We have a solid case against you, and you know it, and we know that your client has already lied on the witness stand when he claimed there were no other accounts that was not on the disclosure sheet, and we know that your client has at least five offshore accounts that each holds approximately two million each. Once this comes out, your client could face possible jail time, plus millions in legal fees. I have no interest in seeing your client in prison stripes. I am only interested in justice for my client. Think it over. Twenty- five million and your client goes on with his business, but you better be quick, for I am recalling Mr. Smithfield as my first witness this afternoon. Mr. Webb then stood and nodded to the lawyer and his client and headed back to the courtroom. I was starved and we had not eaten since dinner the night before.

At 1:15 on the second day of the trial, the judge called for order in the courtroom as the Jury filed in. When it was finally quite Judge McFadden asked Mr. Webb to call his next witness.

Mr. Webb stood, prepared to call Mr. Smithfield once again to the witness chair, When Mr. Barnett Interrupted and asked to approach the bench. The judge motioned for the attorneys forward.

"Judge McFadden, we believe we have reached a settlement 'agreement with the plaintiffs in this case. We would like a few minutes in your chamber to discuss payment and the details of the settlement. The Judge nodded his accent and the attorney's returned to their seats.

The Court will be in recess for twenty minutes. Be back in your seats at 1:45 and judged McFadden banged his gavel.

ZJ CALLOWAY

*"IF THER WERE NO BAD PEOPLE THERE
WOULD BE NO GOOD LAWYERS"*

Benjamin Franklin

19

Settlement Reached

I WAS NOT ALLOWED to enter the Judges Chamber, but Mr. Webb said that the defendants agreed to settle the case for twenty-five million but would not admit negligence. Mr. Webb didn't haggle over that but insisted that the driver of the truck that killed Annabelle Owens be discharged and to recommend to the Union that he never drive again. It was also agreed to by both parties that the case would not be dismissed until the Smithfield Trucking firm had wire transferred the twenty-five million into a special account in the Western Mechanics bank of Tupelo in the name of Marie Ann Owens and the Justin T. Webb law firm. The case lasted only two days. Mr. Webb thanked me and asked me to stop by the next time I was in Tupelo. I called Marie to tell her the news and left a message for her to call. I then pointed my old truck up 51 Highway north to Oxford. I had watched, first-hand how Mr. Webb had taken a small mistake by an experienced Lawyer and turned it into one of the largest settlements, ever, in Mississippi history. Marie Owens would be a very wealthy woman, but it made no difference in easing the pain of losing her daughter.

I didn't make it home again until Easter weekend and stopped by the law firm. Law school was brutal, and I had little time to do anything but study. Mrs. Free announced my presence to Mr. Webb and told me to go on back to his office. He was waiting at the door for me.

"Come in Zack. I had a feeling you might drop by today; I have something for you he handed me the envelope smiling.

He handed me a letter opener from his desk and said, "Go on open it. I opened the letter and pulled out a handwritten letter from Mr. Webb, and inside was a check made out to me in the amount of six hundred and twenty-five thousand dollars, I almost ripped my rompers I was so shocked. "Mr. Webb, what is this for, you don't owe me anything."

"Typical finder's fee; and you deserve every penny. And oh, by the way, Uncle Sam has already got his part. You are a wealthy fellow, Zack, spend it wisely and hurry up and finish law school. I'm ready for a full partner to take the load off these bones."

I was grateful for the money, and yet my life felt empty. I had lost the two loves in my life. Money would not fill the void, but I felt like my financial future was secure.

From the law firm I drove to our home, Momma and Pappy were sitting in the porch swing and Charlie and Robert Lewis sat on the steps, the whole family was laughing at something Robert had said.

Charlie was now fourteen, tall and slender. It seemed that she had grown six inches. She was a beautiful young woman. Robert had grown too. Like his sister he was tall and slender now with a bush of red hair. Charlie and Robert, both met me at the truck, giving me a hug and Charlie as usual gave me a kiss on the cheek. Charlie walked me to the porch with her arm around my waist. Mom and Pop got up. The three years I had spent in school had changed my mom and dad very little. Pappy was getting quite a bit of grey in the temples, but mom had showed practically no sign of aging. They were glad to see me and ushered me inside. Charlie stuck to me like glue.

The family had already eaten supper, but as usual mom had prepared extra, just in case her boys came home for the weekend. I sat at the table with the family around me. They were anxious to hear what I had been doing. I asked Pappy if he would go with me to the farm tomorrow, there was some things I wanted to talk to him about. He said sure, nothing too serious, I hope.

"No, I said, I'm thinking about an investment, and I need your advice and approval."

"I doubt you need my approval; you will soon be twenty-one years old, you can make your own decisions," Pappy said.

I asked the kids if they wanted to go out for ice cream, and of course they were ready. "Do you mind if I invite Penelope?"

For a change Charlie was anxious to see her.

"She calls me sometime and we talk. I like her a lot," she said. "I think she likes you a lot too, but she is afraid because you are so into being a Lawyer and won't have time for a family." Charlie added.

That was news that I hadn't even considered. I wanted a family and would even give up being an attorney if I thought I was neglecting family.

"MABELENE WHY CAN'T YOU BE TRUE; YOU STARTED BACK DOING THE THINGS YOU USED TO DO"

Chuck Berry

20

New Wheels for Penny

"PENNY SAID SHE WOULD meet us at the drugstore at seven."

She came as promised and we ordered Coke floats all around.

"You guys have got to see my new car, he said. well, it's not new but pop bought it for me and restored and repainted it. It is just what I wanted. I think he was tired of driving me to Columbus to the "W" every weekend. He didn't want me riding the bus.

We finished our sodas and Penny invited us for a ride in her black and white two-door 1957 Chevy convertible. She whizzed us around Tupelo and out to the lake and back. It was a beautiful machine. The kids were laughing and having a great time. We were all singing "Maybelline" with Chuck Berry on the radio. She dropped us off at the drugstore and roared away after she asked me to come by her place the next day. She said there was something she wanted to talk about.

The next morning after breakfast Pappy and I left for the farm in my old truck.

"I have to swing by the bank to make a deposit," I said. I got a check from the Webb law firm for helping With Marie Owens Lawsuit against Smithfield Trucking in Memphis.

"I read about that lawsuit in the paper, Pappy said but it never said how much they settled for."

"Twenty-five million, I said off handedly. Mr. Webb gave me a finder's fee for bringing the case to him and he wants me to join his firm when I graduate from Law school, and maybe eventually take over the firm.

"Sounds like a mighty good offer. Mr. Webb is a mighty good man, and a fine lawyer," Pappy said.

"I agree, I said. Wish you could have seen him in court. The opposing lawyer made a small mistake and Mr. Webb had him on the ropes in five minutes."

We drove on to the farm and stopped long enough at the barn to see Lucas. Today he was shoeing a pair of red mules and a black mare. The weather was hot, and Lucas took his bandana and wiped away sweat that was running down his face from his temples. He came to the truck and shook my hand and said he was glad to see me. I asked how school was going with Charlie.

"Graduated, "he said flatly. "She said she had taught me about all she could teach me with her education. She still brings me books to read, and sometimes I read to her; that girl is a real prize!"

"We are going to saddle up and ride out for a spell." He waved his hand and bent over with a hoof between his legs and began nailing on a horseshoe.

Pappy and I saddled up and rode out to where Willy and I had built the new gate. I got off, opened the gate and led the Dapple Grey through, and Pappy followed on the Black.

We rode across the green pasture in near Knee-high grass, to the ridge where Penny and I had ridden Many months before. We dismounted and looked across the expanse.

"How many acres in this place Pappy?"

"Four hundred," he answered, looking at me sideways with his eyes squinted. Why?"

"Would you sell it to me?"

Pappy was silent as he looked at me in a questioning way, that only pappy could do.

"Well, I intended to give most all this property to you and Willy when you two had finished college. Why would you want to buy it, now, and the next question, that I knew was coming, and what would you buy it with? You don't even have a job."

'You are right, I don't have a job, but I do have money and quite a bit of it."

"Enough to pay forty dollars per acre for this piece of land?"

"Yes."

"And why this piece."

"This is where I want to live. I want to build my home and raise a family right here on this ridge."

"I don't know. Pappy said. Let me talk to Willy and your Momma. I will let you know before you go back to school."

"I also want you to help me buy a better truck. I want to keep this one and give it to Charlie when she is old enough to drive if its ok with you and Momma."

"Trying to buy land and a new truck: must have been a heck of a finder's fee." Pappy opined.

"It was," I said as I mounted up for the ride to the barn.

Twenty minutes later we were at the Chevrolet/GMC dealership looking over their selection. I picked out a Chevy truck almost identical to the one Willy had bought three years before. It belonged to the owner of the dealership with only four thousand miles on the Odometer. He sold it to me for nine hundred dollars, cash. No trade.

"I figured when I saw you and your son come on the lot this morning that you had come after the rest of my hide. I started to hide in the cellar, so what can I do for you Mr. Callaway?"

"The boy here wants to upgrade. Says he can pay cash for a good deal."

I walked around the lot and looked over the new ones which listed for over two thousand dollars. Two expensive for my pocketbook I told him. I was hoping to find a good used one like my brother's. Like that one over there. I pointed to a light blue Chevy.

"Well, that is my personal truck, but I guess I would be willing to part with it for the right price. It's only got 4800 miles on and has only been serviced twice. The tires are good, and it has a good radio and Heater, and chrome all around and gear shift on the steering column."

What's the right price?" I asked.

"Oh, I guess about twelve hundred," he lamented.

"Make it a thousand and we've got a deal."

"Give me an hour to service it and fill the tank and get the title. You have a month warranty on everything, or to return it if you don't like it and I'll give your money back."

"Pappy and I drove back toward the house, and he could contain himself no longer.

"Just how much finder's fee did Mr. Webb pay you?"

"Between me and you, Pappy. Six hundred and twenty-five thousand dollars."

"Holy crap!" Pappy shouted, are you kidding me."

"Nope," I pulled the bank deposit from shirt and handed it to him.

"That old man Webb has gone plum nuts giving away that much money to someone he's not even related to."

"Don't think he's crazy, he will net over five million out of the settlement and Mrs. Owens will net close to seventeen Million. She is now a very wealthy woman."

"Well, be careful with your money, that would last most people a lifetime, but easy money has a way of slipping away. Easy-come, Easy-Go, the old folks say."

I knew that Pappy was right, and I was going to be very careful with the new-found wealth. I would spend some on the farm to build a house for me and my son, and a new barn. Beyond that my job at the law firm would provide all the income that I needed.

I DON'T NEED A KNIGHT IN SHINING ARMOR,
A NICE BOY IN A PICKUP TRUCK WILL DO.

Unknown Source

21

New Wheels and Money to Spend

AFTER LUNCH I DROVE to Penney's house across town, and asked her if she would she like to take a ride in my new truck?

"In that old heap, she laughed, nodding at my truck. Think it will make it there and back? she said laughing."

"Smart Aleck."

"Wait, let me tell Pop we're driving around for a while. She went into the house and was back in a few minutes. She wore jeans and a Tee which really showed her figure. She was beautiful, happy and smiling. I was liking her more and more every time I saw her. But I could not, for the life of me, figure out if she had any romantic interest in me. That was irritating as hell.

"You said that you had something you wanted to talk about last night. What's up?"

"Well, I'm not sure you are going to like what I'm going to tell you," she said.

I think my heart skipped about five beats; I was prepared for the worse.

"I got a call from Naught McCullough. In fact, I have had several calls. He is coming by in three weeks to see his mother on his way to a new assignment in San Diego. He is to be here for at least two years but has been promised the Recruiting Sergeant's position in Columbus when the position comes open again. He asked me to go out with him and I said I would. Please don't hate me Zack, I like him and didn't want to hurt him." I am sure it will just be a one-time thing," she added.

"I don't hate you Penny, I know I haven't been able to see you much, and I don't blame you for seeing other people. I just simply have not had time for romance these last four years. I hope I can still see you when I come home though.

"Sure Zack, you are a really great guy and I enjoy being with you, anytime you have the time."

Outward I was calm but, on the inside, I felt I had fell face first in a pile of cow manure. There was more to this than it appeared.

Sunday Willy came driving in about nine o'clock. He had work to do on campus but was taking Monday off, and a retired Colonial was guest speaking to the class on Military discipline."

I drove back to Ole Miss late Sunday afternoon. Pappy said he had not been able to talk to Willy and could not give me an answer on buying the property until he did, but he did not really want to sell me the property, since he was going to deed it to us when we graduated anyhow.

I left a message for Marie when I got to my apartment, but she didn't return my call until the next morning. She called just as I was about to sit down for a bowl of corn flakes, and a cold donut.

"Sorry about not calling last night but was not feeling very well and was already in bed when you called."

"How long have you been ill," I asked.

"Just a couple of days she said. "It's probably nothing but fatigue. I have really been busy in my job. I thought that after three years, the job would get easier and I could take time off, but the company keeps buying banks and the load just gets heavier.

"Well, you are a very rich lady now. You don't have to work. Quit the job and come back to Tupelo. I pleaded.

"No Zack, we have already been through this. I need the job to keep my sanity and beside that I have already remodeled my home there to rent out."

"Well, if you don't feel better soon, you need to see a doctor."

"I will do that," she said. I will call if I see a doctor.

She didn't call for more than a month, it was frustrating, but there was nothing I could do. Marie was gone and was not going to be coming back.

I didn't make it home again until the end of the summer session. I needed a break and decided to take the time between semesters and fly from Memphis to St. Louis and watch the Cardinals in a three-game series against the Dodgers. During the day I took tours of the city and ate at the best restaurants. I returned to Oxford after five days feeling much better, but the emptiness in my heart was still there. It was a void I could not seem to fill.

*"I SUPPOSE IF YOU ARE GOING TO MAKE
A CAREER OF BREAKING THE LAWS, YOU
MIGHT AS WELL LEARN THEM."*

Michelle Meade

22

Ole Miss 1962 Integration

MY SECOND YEAR OF Law school was one for the history books. James Meredith, a Black Man, and a native Mississippian who was attending school at Jackson State College had applied for admission to Law school on three occasions but was rejected on all three attempts. He then filed suit in Federal Court, asking the court to order the University to admit him. The suit ended up before the United States Supreme Court. The essence of the suit was that he was rejected because he was black. The Court agreed with Meredith and ordered the University to admit him at once. When the governor of Mississippi, Paul Johnson, refused to obey the order the Attorney General of the United States, Robert Kennedy ordered three thousand National Guard troops from across the country to Oxford to enforce the court order. President John Kennedy then ordered another six thousand Federal troops to the town. Kennedy went on National television to ask for calm but assured the country that the court order would be enforced. Protesters rioted when confronted with the military presence. Two people were killed and several hundred injured when the military moved to quell the upheaval. The news media essentially made a mountain out of a molehill, where the riot was concerned. There was little damage to the university or downtown Oxford.

Many of us watched the affair from the steps of the Law School as events unfolded. By morning the rioters were gone, and the military was in full control, Mr. Meredith entered the law school accompanied by a bevy of United state marshals. He officially became a student on October 2, 1962. From all accounts, few students took part in the riots, but were blamed for much of the disorder.

Anyone who was an Ole Miss football fan hardly gave thought to the turmoil surrounding the James Meredith issues. The Ole Miss Rebels were a football powerhouse, and the fans were ready to watch their team in action. Willy and I had student tickets to every home game, and one in Memphis. When the season was over the team had won the SEC championship and a bid to the sugar bowl. They were also crowned National champions. Other major occurrences overshadowed anything that was happening on campus. William Faulkner passed away in July. But Mississippians barely noticed his passing, for there were race riots all across the southland that dominated every news cycle on television. Martin Luther King, a young preacher from Atlanta, led marches across the South, protesting racial discrimination. The racial divide was deep in the state but most of the turmoil was brought on by the power brokers and political leaders, and not everyday citizens. Most Mississippians were peace loving and gentle folks and despised the way its leaders were acting. It was a tumultuous period for Mississippi and for the nation.

When school started back in January the campus was calm but Federal troops continue to roam the campus for several months. And we got down to business of studying Law. When I entered the final semester in January, I had already taken the bar exam and passed. Months later, President John Kennedy was assassinated in Dallas by Lee Harvey Oswald, and while the nation mourned, racial demonstrations continued throughout the South and across the nation. It was a difficult time. There were protest marches across the state, but fortunately Tupelo, however, escaped much of the strife that plagued most of the country.

I rarely called Marie Owens but at the beginning of spring break I received a call from a lady who claimed to be Marie's housekeeper.

She said Marie was very sick and wanted me to come to Seattle to see her. That she had booked a flight for me on Delta Air Lines out of Memphis. She said Marie had been admitted to the Virginia Mason hospital in Seattle the week before, she was very ill and her condition had continued to deteriorate to a point that her doctors had said it was time to call in her family, for she was near death. Beverly, the housekeeper said that Marie needed to see me immediately. I did not hesitate. I put on Khaki pants and a sport jacket, packed another suit of clothes in a carry-on handbag and headed for the airport in Memphis, seventy-five miles away. Nine hours later the Douglas DC 8 was parking at the terminal after stops in Kansas City and Omaha. I waited outside for a taxi in a cold mist, and in minutes I was on my way to see Marie after four and a half years.

*"TO WORRY ABOUT AGE DIFFERENCE WHERE
LOVE IS CONCERNED IS A FOOLISH PURSUIT,
FOR TOMORROW IS NO GUARANTEE; LOVE
EACH DAY AS IF IT WERE THE LAST"*

RC

23

Saying Goodbye

MY HEART WAS BEATING wildly as the cab pulled to the curb in front of the downtown hospital. Inside I went straight to the information desk and was told that Marie was on the fourth floor. When I stepped off the elevator, the smell if alcohol and dysentery was strong. Marie was to be in room 420. Room 420 was a CCU. My heart sank further, I asked the nurse outside if I could see her. She asked me my name and looked at her clip board, got up and told me to follow her. She led me through to a narrow hallway through double doors into a ward of rooms divided with only pull curtains.

Behind the curtains Marie lay sleeping with Iv's dripping fluid into her vein. She was on oxygen to help her breathe. The nurse brought in a padded lounge chair and told me to stay as long as I liked. The nurse left the room, and I went to Marie and kissed her tenderly. She opened her eyes and reached for me; her eyes filled with tears. I sat on the side of the bed and held her in my arms for a few seconds.

"Oh Zack, she whispered, I am so sick, but I had to see you long enough to tell you why I left Tupelo, and to tell you that I love you one last time. I was diagnosed with lung cancer two weeks ago and it has spread throughout the rest of my body. There is a package over there with things in it that I want you to read tonight for they tell me I only hours left. Kiss me again dear Zack for I am so tired I must sleep."

I kissed her again and held her in my arm until her doctor and his nurse entered the little room. She was asleep when the doctor examined her briefly, listening to her heart, and checking her pulse. He made no comment when he left the room.

Marie Owens died peacefully on April 2, 1963, at 11:45 PM. She was thirty-nine years old. I was sitting beside her, holding her hand with her doctor and nurse standing beside her. I bowed my head, said a prayer and wept, my heart breaking.

The Doctor came to me and explained that the cancer was fast moving and just consumed her, "We tried radiation therapy, he said, but nothing we did could abate the spread. There was simply nothing we could do but to try and make her last hours comfortable."

The doctor said the hospital would see to the task of getting in touch with the mortuary. He said she had left instructions for that.

It was near midnight when I checked into a hotel next to the hospital. I was very tired but sat at a small desk and opened the large package- size envelope that she had left me. On the very top was a handwritten letter that she had written to me two days earlier

March 31, 1963

My Dearest Zack,

If you are reading this, you know that I am no longer with you. I have a few things I must tell you that are of great importance to me. The reason I left Tupelo was that I was pregnant with your baby. Zack, you have a son who is now almost five years old. His name is Zachery James Calloway; we call him ZJ.

You will find his birth records and a few pictures of him taken at various times over these past five years. He is a precious child and very bright and I know you will love him as I have. He is with my friend

and live-in housekeeper, Beverly Dalton. She will be expecting you. You will find the address enclosed. Also, you will find the deed to my house in Tupelo deeded over to you. I also took the liberty to have most of my cash assets transferred to your bank account in Tupelo. Since you were banking with our bank in Tupelo, I was able to get your account number and deposit the money directly to your checking account. It amounts to more than thirteen million dollars. You are a very wealthy man, but I pray that you will raise our child as you have been raised and not as a wealthy aristocrat. Use your wealth to help the less fortunate and not to spoil our child.

The rest of my assets I have willed to Beverly. She has been a Godsend to me, and I have left her enough that she can live comfortably from a life insurance policy I have had for some time. There are other papers you will need in a box in my apartment. You will also find the rest of Anna's diaries that she has kept since the sixth grade.

One last thing I want you to know: I loved you deeply when we made love and I learned I was carrying you child. However, I did not want you to feel like I had kept you from pursuing your dreams to be a lawyer, so I made my mind to raise the child on my own. I know now that I was wrong about that. We could have been together for these five years sharing our love for each other. I have never been sorry that we made love and I had your child. He has been a joy in my life as was Annabelle.

Have a good life Zack, find someone to love and love each day like it was your last, and take care of our son.

With Love
Marie Ann

24

Meeting My Son

FOR THE NEXT HOUR I cried, before fatigue overtook me, and I slept until the morning sun was casting rays across my bed. I quickly showered, dressed in jeans and a Polo, and called for a cab. Ten minutes later we were at the street address that Marie had provided. I was scared to death to meet my own son. My hands were trembling when I summoned enough courage to ring the doorbell. Shortly, I could hear small feet padding toward the door. The door opened and there stood my son who was a spitting image of me when I was five. Behind him was a pretty lady that appeared to be in her late forties or early fifty's. I held out my hand to her and introduced myself. And I said kneeling, "I figure this is ZJ."

"Yes, and we have been expecting you, Mr. Calloway. The hospital called Just after twelve last night. So sad," she added. "Marie was probably the sweetest lady I have ever known."

"I have just made coffee, why don't you sit at the table, and we can talk. Can I fix you something to eat? I made cinnamon rolls yesterday and that's what we had for breakfast."

"Yes, I am hungry. I haven't eaten since yesterday at noon. I grabbed a hotdog when we had a stopover in Omaha."

"I'll heat them up for a couple of minutes in the warmer, they are much better hot."

ZJ sat beside me, and Beverly poured him a glass of milk and sat a plate and fork in front of him. Minutes later she scooped me two huge cinnamon rolls and a small one for ZJ. He looked up at me as if to say, "are you really going to eat two of those?"

"So, ZJ, what do you like to do?" Do you have a game that you really love to Play?"

"I like baseball," he said, "I want to be a baseball player when I grow up."

"You know I love baseball, too. My brother and I played baseball in high school. His name is Willy. We will have to go together to watch a game."

"Are you, my daddy? ZJ asked out of the blue. Momma said when she got sick that you would be coming to get me to go and live with you. Where do you live?"

"I live in Mississippi. A town called Tupelo, but right now I'm in college for two more months, and then we will live in our house in Tupelo."

"Do you mind if I go watch cartoons now?" He asked.

"No, that would be ok, I need to talk with Miss Beverly for a few minutes."

When he left the table, he said excuse me and then ran to the sofa in the other room. I asked Beverly if she had a family.

"My husband and young daughter were killed in an auto accident twenty years ago. I have a sister in San Diego. I have only seen her a few times since the death of my husband. That is all the family that I have."

"You have been with Marie for how long?"

"Since she moved here nearly five years ago. I needed a job badly and she took a chance on me. She may have saved me from being on the street. She has told me a little about you and the reason that she left Mississippi. She said you were the kindest man that she ever knew and would make a great father. The age difference between you two, she felt was something that people would not accept."

"Yes, I know, it kept us from being together. But all that is in the past. I now have to focus on raising my son. I was wondering if you might consider being my housekeeper. I need someone at least until I finish school. I will match whatever you are now earning and pay all expenses to make the move. We have a nice home in a good neighborhood, and if you choose to, we will make it permanent."

"Let me think on it overnight and I will let you know in the morning."

"Do you own a car?" I asked her.

"No, I don't drive I take the bus when I shop or need to go into the city."

"That will not be a problem. We have a neighborhood grocery within walking distance, and I will provide you with an ample expense allowance for food and other necessities. Please consider the offer carefully, my son and I need you, and it is obvious that he loves you."

"I have only been out of Washington state twice in my whole life. I don't know about going to Mississippi, but I will consider it carefully and pray about it." She said. "I love your son dearly and hate the thought of being separated from him."

"I got up and thanked her for the food and coffee and told her I needed to go to the mortuary to be sure the instructions she left me are fulfilled."

I said goodbye to ZJ and told him I would be back by noon. "You might want to help Miss Beverly pack your clothes and a few toys for our flight to Mississippi."

"Ok," he said then asked, "Is it a long way to Mississippi?"

"Yes, it is a long way, but I think you will really like it when we get there. We have horses to ride and a big pond to catch fish."

"I have never been fishing," he said, "but I want to go. Will you show me how?"

"I sure will, and I like to fish, too. I will teach you how to ride horses too. I have to go now, but I'll be back soon." I reached down and tussled his hair and have him a hug and went to the door. He followed me until I was outside. The cab came seconds later, and I was dreading going to the mortuary. It would be the last time I would see her, for Marie had given instruction that her casket was to remain closed until she was buried and that I was the only person to review her remains.

One of the employees at the funeral parlor greeted me when I approached the business office. She went over the instructions that Marie had given them. They had prepared the body for burial and was to ship the body by airfreight to Memphis and the Funeral home in Columbus would send a hearse to take care of the grave-side service and burial. She asked if I would like to view her corpse now, and I nodded yes. She then led me from the business office down a very narrow hallway to an area where bodies of deceased were awaiting a funeral service in the funeral home's chapel or waiting to be shipped to other locations. The area was ice cold and there were no trappings of elegance as were the chapels and visitation areas.

She led me to a copper-colored caskets with gold trimmings. Without fanfare or comment she opened the casket and then stepped back away from the body so that I could draw close, for the room was crowded with bodies.

In death as in life Marie was a beautiful woman. Marie had lost her hair during radiation therapy and the funeral home had provided her with a hairpiece. I asked her to have them remove it the wig because it took from her lovely face. She said that she would have a mortician come and remove it. She went to a wall phone, spoke a few words and moments a man in a white lab coat came to the casket and removed the wig. I thanked him, but he only nodded as he left the room. I stepped close to Marie and touched the back of my hand to her face and whispered goodbye. I told the matron that she could close the casket, and we made our way back to the office. I asked her if there was a private place with a phone where I could make a few calls. I had not called my parents or Charlie to let them know about Marie's passing or that they now had a grandchild. I dialed the operator and asked to place a collect call to AC Calloway in Tupelo Mississippi. Momma answered the phone but when the operator spoke, she handed the phone off to Pappy.

"Will you accept a collect call from Zack Calloway."

"Er, why, well yes he finally stuttered."

"Sorry Pappy, but It was important that I talk to you before I talked to anyone else. I am in Seattle, Washington. Marie Owens passed away last night just before midnight. Her housekeeper called me yesterday morning and told me that Marie was very sick and wanted to see me. I left immediately. She had a form of lung cancer that consumed her body quickly. They are flying her body to Memphis tomorrow and there will be a graveside service at Friendship Cemetery in Columbus on Friday."

"I'm sorry to hear that," Pappy said, "she was a lovely, and sweet person, but I have a feeling there is more to the story of why you are in Seattle".

"Yes. there is more to the story. A lot more. Marie and I have a son. I will be bringing him to Tupelo with me tomorrow.

"I want you to tell Momma and Charlie. Charlie will be devastated at the news. She was crazy about Marie, you know.

There's something else I need you to do for me."

"Just name it son," Pappy said.

"Marie deeded me and our son her house in Tupelo. ZJ ad I will be living there when I return. I need you, Momma and Charlie to go over and be sure the place is clean and is stocked with groceries, you know, clean sheets and towels and all that kind of thing, make sure there is electricity and water. No one has lived in the house for five years so it may not be in the best of shape. You will find a key to the front door in the cup holder on the porch swing"

"I would like for the family to attend the service on Friday in Columbus. There will be an obituary in the Journal tomorrow morning. I'm sorry for the trouble I've caused but once You see your grandson, I think you and Mom will forgive me."

"Of course, we will forgive you and we will wait anxiously to meet our grandson. Your mother will be tickled pink to have a grandson to spoil rotten. What is the boy's name?"

"His name is Zachery James, but we call him ZJ."

25

A New Home

WE LANDED IN MEMPHIS a little after noon on Thursday. Beverly had agreed to come and be my housekeeper and Nanny at least until I graduate from Law school in May but would not commit to a longer term until she could try Mississippi on for size. I picked my truck up at the Airport parking deck, and headed down highway 51 to Batesville and then highway 6 East to Oxford and the campus at Ole Miss. Beverly and ZJ helped me load my few belongings into the bed of my truck. I left my landlord a note that I would not be back, but I left a check which would pay through the end of May and that would fulfill my rental agreement.

We arrived at our new home in Tupelo by mid-afternoon. I found the key under the doormat, and we all went inside. The place was spotless. There was new carpet on the floor, and new drapes on the windows and new paint inside and outside. Marie had seen to it that the place was kept in good condition, even though she no longer lived there. It was a two bedroom–two bath house. The master bedroom had an adjoining bath, and I told Beverly to take that one and ZJ and I would take the other and would share the bathroom in the hallway. Beverly protested though and we finally agreed for the boys to take the master bedroom. I called Momma to let them know we were home and five

143

minutes later the whole family was pulling into the yard. Charlie was the first on out of truck. She hugged me and kissed me on the cheek. She had turned eighteen in May and was as beautiful as ever. She was a woman now, in every way. She was tall, slender and as graceful as a butterfly.

The family was all over ZJ and he hit it off especially well with Robert and Charlie. Momma had him in her arms in minutes and he was talking non-stop to Pappy. Momma said she was making dinner for us tonight, so we could get to know everyone. Beverly was also taken to my family. She and Momma talked as if they were just old friends that had not seen each other for a while.

I had worried some about how Momma and Pappy would accept ZJ, but it was needless worry, for it was plain they were going to love him.

The obituary was published for Marie Thursday Morning.

> *Marie Ann Owens recently of Seattle Washington, and formerly from Tupelo, passed away at 11:45 PM Monday at Virginia Mason hospital in Seattle. She is survived by many friends and one child, Zachery James Calloway of Tupelo. She is preceded in death by her husband. Roy Don Owens, her parents, Mr. and Mrs. James Coleman, and her daughter Annabelle Marie Owens. Graveside Service for family and friends will be at 11:00 AM at Friendship Cemetery in Columbus. The service will be officiated by Assistant Pastor of First Presbyterian Church, Doctor Ralph Nelson.*
>
> *Marie was a long-time employee of Mechanics and Builders Bank of Tupelo, working her way up from teller to CFO of banking operations in Mississippi, Tennessee, and Seattle Washington. Marie was a graduate of Lee High School in Columbus and earned her CPA through the University of Mississippi Extension program. Marie had no other living relatives.*

Friday Morning, we left Tupelo at nine thirty, ZJ. Beverly, Charlie and me in my truck. Charlie had just turned eighteen and was dressed in a solid black dress with a very small cross on a thin gold chain around her neck. Momma had seen to it that she was dressed appropriately. She was stunning—her long red hair in ringlets nearly to her waist. Charlie holding the boy in her lap all the way. Pappy, Momma, Robert and Lucas in Pappy's truck. We arrived at the ancient cemetery just an hour later. The funeral home had set up a large tent at the burial site and a dozen, or so, people had already gathered out of the morning sun. There was a row of chairs set up for family members, but of course she had none but her son. I asked Angela to sit with my family on the front row. The service lasted a little more than twenty- five minutes, and most of that taken by the president of Mechanics and Builders Bank who gave a glowing testimony to her work ethic and her intellect. Dr. Nelson talked about the sorrow in her life, losing her husband in the war, and then her beautiful daughter. But she had joy too, he said, with the birth of her son and the love of her many friends. The choir of First Presbyterian sang Amazing Grace and there was a prayer, and the service of Marie Ann Owens was over. She had been one of two loves in my life, but my name was never mentioned. However, my heart was crying out, "why God did you take this beautiful person?"

Beverly took ZJ to the truck and I waited until workmen lowered Marie's body into the grave and covered it with black Mississippi soil. A light Magnolia wind blew from the southwest as I walked away.

The next two months were difficult, having to leave my son and drive to Oxford each day for classes and then back, gave me a bit of a guilt complex. I was thankful that I had finished my six-week training in the Air Force. I had been assigned duties at The Guard unit in Tupelo but would have to spend six weeks on active duty at England Air Force Base in Louisiana for the next three years.

*"THE MINUTE YOU READ SOMETHING YOU
DON'T UNDERSTAND, YOU CAN ALMOST BE
CERTAIN IT WAS WRITTEN BY A LAWYER."*

Will Rogers

26

Man of the Law

MY FIRST CLIENTS

I GRADUATED FROM THE University of Mississippi school of
Law on May 15, 1964. I walked in the graduation ceremony through
the beautiful Grove, in June simply because I had graduated with
honors and had place near the top of the class.

I went to work on Monday after the Saturday graduation. Momma
and Pappy had bought me a new leather briefcase and Charlie had
bought picture frames and had my diploma and my law license ready
to be hung. I climbed the stairs to The Law Offices of Webb, Calloway,
and associates. The whole crew was waiting to greet me and applauded
loudly when I entered. There was a bottle of champaign on the desk,
but Mr. Webb said it would have to wait for I had clients waiting to see
me in my new office. I walked down the hallway to a small conference
room that had been remodeled into a nice office with a new mahogany
desk with a leather padded matching chair. A new set of Mississippi
Law books lined the shelves behind the desk. A copy of my law license
had already been hung on the wall. There were two visitor chairs in

front of the desk and a matching leather loveseat along the right wall. Waiting in the chairs was Jannie McCullough and Joe Webb. I was surprised to say the least. Mrs. McCullough stood, and I gave her a hug and I grasped the calloused hand of my friend Joe Webb. I walked around the desk and sat down.

"Can I get you coffee or something to drink," I asked.

"No thanks," they both answered in unison.

"Well, what brings you two to see a lawyer, you rob a bank, Joe?"

Mrs. McCullough laughed, as she said no. "Joe and I want to get married, and I need to get a divorce from my husband, Darren Naught McCullough. He deserted us when my oldest boy was seven, and the youngest was five years old. I haven't seen him since. He called a few times wanting me to give him money, but of course I had none to give. I hope it can be done without ever seeing the man again."

"Do you have a last known address? We must try to locate him to advise him that he has a right to contest the divorce. Which is unlikely since desertion is one of the reasons for the divorce request. An uncontested divorce usually takes a little over sixty days; contested longer."

"What will it cost?"

"One dollar is my fee, but the firm usually charges a hundred for an uncontested divorce. In your case we have waived all the fees.

"You can't live on those kinds of wages, Zack. You know I am able to pay." Joe asserted.

''Yeah, I know but my Pappy would whip me with a hickory limb if he knew I charged you for anything. You and Mrs. McCullough are two of Momma and Pappy's closest friends. They love you both, and so do I. Give me five minutes and I will have a few papers for Mrs. McCullough to sign and then you can be on your way. I will take care of everything from now until you have a court date."

Mrs. McCullough signed the required paperwork, and Mrs. Free typed a letter to send to her husband whose last known address was General Delivery, Grove, Texas.

I asked the newly engaged couple to stay and have champaign with us, but they refused. I knew that neither of them touched liquor of any kind. I took the dollar that Janie paid me; it would be framed for my wall. I wrote her a receipt and kept a duplicate for my records.

I watched them through the hallway window until they embraced and kissed on the street below. It was a not so subtle, message that they were a couple now and it was no secret. I smiled at the thought of the two finally finding love and wondered if I would someday find a love that would fill this empty place inside me. I wondered if the sadness that I felt now would ever end.

*FROM THE HALLS OF MONTEZUMA TO THE
SHORES OF TRIPOIE, WE WILL FIGHT OUR
NATION'S BATTLES IN THE AIR, ON THE
LAND AND OVER THE SEAS……………..*

Marine Battle Hymn

27

Sgt. Naught McCullough
Takes Leave

SERGEANT NAUGHT MCCULLOUGH BOARDED the
shuttle bus that would take him from Paris Island South Carolina where
he had served as a technical advisor to new recruits, to Savannah Georgia,
where he would catch a Greyhound Bus to Tupelo. He had taken two
weeks leave time to visit his mother whom he had not seen in more than
two years. He was on his way to a new assignment in San Diego, where
he was supposed to serve a two-year tour. His Commanding Officer
had promised him he would be assigned recruiting duties in North
Mississippi and would be stationed at Oxford, New Albany, or Tupelo.
With the Marines, however, orders were day to day and in many cases,
orders came with no notice,

Naught had been talking to Penny Johnson on the phone lately,
and he was hoping she still had some feelings for him, and he wanted to
rekindle that relationship. He had been gone nearly eight years and had
been all over the world. He wondered if she had any feelings at all for

him. He knew she had gone out with Zack Calloway, but she assured him there was nothing but friendship going on.

It was about an hour drive to Savannah and from there a sixteen-hour bus ride to Tupelo. At the station in Savannah the driver unloaded his two bags on the platform, and he waited at the coffee counter for his bus from somewhere south to pull into the station. His bus was supposed to arrive in Tupelo the next morning just before eleven. There would be stops at Macon, Atlanta, and Birmingham and a dozen other small towns along the way. He could have taken the train, but it was an even longer ride and the bus was much more comfortable.

It wasn't long until the bus pulled into the station and took on a half dozen new passenger. Nate was a slim six-foot, two inch a hundred-and-ninety-five-pound soldier and looked every bit of the fighting man the marines were famous for. He had seen action around the globe, and he proudly displayed a chest full of medals. He harbored no ill feelings toward Zack Calloway for going out with Penny, Zack was his friend, and he knew that he would not have gone out with Penny if he thought there was something between Penny and himself. Zack was not that kind of man.

The bus stopped in Macon for no more than five minutes and took on only one new passenger. The bus was less than half full. Darkness had settled over the southland and a fine mist began to fall. Naught, using his carry-on bag as a pillow stretched his long body out on the bench seat and closed his eyes. His mind swept back to his first time in combat. His unit had been sent to replace a unit along 38th parallel Northeast of Soule, and approximately twenty-five miles north of Hogenson. There was also an army tank division backing the Marines along with a unit of heavy artillery. His unit set up camp with fifty caliber machine guns, along a one mile stretch of rugged mountain terrain, that was snow covered but was now almost solid sheets of ice. It was so far, below zero that thermometers often froze, and it was impossible to stay warm. Naught had bought the heaviest pair of long-handles at the post exchange that he could buy before they shipped out, but it was little help against the cold wind that never seem to stop blowing. Once they had set up their defenses, guards took turns walking in quarter-mile stretches. The war had been essentially over for five years. It was a war that never was a war. The cease fire had halted the conflict, but North Korean soldiers would occasionally come across the line and capture American soldiers, take them to one of the many prisons just North of the 38th Parallel, and use them for propaganda purposes. The second night after they had made camp, four soldiers had captured two of his marine comrades and started north with them.

Although American troops had orders to never cross into North Korea, his commanding officers, Major Benjamin Lee, called a small group of his unit together and explained what happened. He told Naught, who had just earned his Sergeant stripes, and the rest of the group that he could not order them to go after the men, but if volunteers wanted to go and bring them back. He would have to swear the volunteers had acted on their own. When the Officer had left for his tent, Naught asked for three volunteers to go with him. Every hand in the unit went up. Naught picked three that he knew would follow his orders and would put their life on the line if needed. Naught went to the captain and asked permission for he and the three men he had selected to go a little further north and see if there was sign of the two missing men.

The Major went to his footlocker and took out four 45 caliber Colts with screw on silencers and four wires. Every Marine had been trained in the use of a wire, which was nothing but a piano string with handles on both ends. The wire, in the hands of a strong and skilled soldier could decapitate an enemy soldier in one second flat. He handed the equipment to Naught. He said he didn't think the soldiers would be in much of a hurry once they crossed back into North Korea. He saluted Naught and told him good Luck and be careful.

Naught and the three soldiers, two Privates, and a Corporal, headed north. The tracks were easy to follow by the light of the moon, in the snow and Ice. They crossed into North Korea an hour later. There were no fences on this stretch of rough mountainous terrain. Just a couple strands of barbed wire to mark the separation of the two nations. The North Koreans had set their defenses much like the Americas and, guards walked their post at shorter intervals, but the guards had built a fire half-way in between their posts, and every now and then would stop to warm by the fire. This was a stroke of luck for Naught and his men. They waited and watched through field telescopes, until the guards sat down for a foot warming. Naught had his men to belly crawl until they were out of sight of the guards. They wormed their way across enemy lines through scrub brush and deep cervices until they were well behind enemy lines. The captain had been right, the enemy soldiers were in no hurry, and Naught and his men overtook them within an hour. They had built a small fire, for there was little wood to be found to fuel a big one. Naught and his men could hear the soldiers laughing. Naught ordered his men to stay put while he tried to get a look. He belly-crawled. staying low in the brush. They had tied the two Marines to a broken-down half-track. They had stripped off their jackets and shirts and were taking turns burning the soldiers with cigarettes. The Marines, however, only flinched but without clothing they would not last until morning. He ordered his men forward until they were within twenty feet of the enemy. Suddenly, one of the American soldiers started cursing the Koreans, and spitting at them. Naught figured that was a signal that the Americans had spotted them in the brush and was doing his best to distract his captors. All four of the Koreans got up from the fire and started beating them with their Billy clubs. That was all the time they needed. He held up his wire and ordered the men to attack. In fifteen seconds the four Koreans lay dead, and the American Marines were free from their captors. They stripped the Koreans of their clothes, guns and ammunition. One of the Marines had suffered a broken arm and burns all over his torso, but he could walk, and the six men headed back south the way they had come.

'Naught ordered his men to use the wire and attach it to the men they had killed, that they were going to drag the dead soldiers back below the 38th parallel. The way naught figured it, if the soldiers were in South Korean territory his commanding officers would be in the clear. However, the 38th parallel was more than a mile away and they had to get the job done before thy lost the benefit of darkness. All they had to do was get back to base camp without getting killed or starting another war. They were belly crawling taking turns dragging the dead men, when they suddenly heard a vehicle coming their way. They laid low until the vehicle, carrying two soldiers was within fifty feet, it was time to act or be run over by a half track.

He ordered the men to get ready and held up the 45 with a silencer and motioned them forward. When the halftrack was only yards when the four marines rose up and commenced firing. The driver was killed by Naught's shot through the windshield. The passenger tried to leap from the vehicle but was shot dead by Private Levinson. The truck careened toward Naught, and he had to dive to keep from being hit. Naught ordered all the dead soldiers be loaded into the back of the half-track, and for his men to load up too, He took the wheel with Private Levinson riding shotgun. He hoped to make it to the guard post before guards realized it was not their own soldiers in the truck,

"Let's get out of here before we have more trouble. Someone will miss these soldiers, and we won't be hard to follow. When we get to the guard- post we just keep driving like we knew where we were going, if they recognize that something is wrong, we give this truck the gas and try to make it back across the border. It was a bold and dangerous move, but it worked. Naught and the Corporal put on the hats of the dead officers and headed South. North Korean guards did not recognize a problem until it was too late. The guards fired no shots before the Marines had made it back to the Marine unit.

"Naught and Corporal Levinson were awarded the Bronze Star, for bravery in thwarting an apparent attempt by six North Korean soldiers to cross the 38th Parallel apparently to capture marines walking guard duty. Sergeant McCullough and Corporal Livingston killed the six North Korean soldiers who had taken two marines but did not make it back to North Korea."

Naught knew that was not what really happened, but it was a version that would satisfy the top brass.

28

Heading Home

NAUGHT WAS AWAKENED BY the driver's intercom when the bus was pulling into Atlanta Station. "One hour layover for refueling, the driver said, they serve good food in the station café."

Sergeant McCullough had been sleeping for six hours, but his neck felt like he had been hung from a White oak. He was hungry as a woodpecker with a headache, and the smell of food made him forget the soreness in his neck. He went inside and ate.

McCullough stepped off the bus at 11:05 in Tupelo. He had phoned his mother, and she was supposed to pick him up at the station. However, she was not there, so he picked up his bags and took a seat on a bench in front of the station and waited. A half-hour later she still had not come, so he went to the pay phone, dropped a dime in the slot and dialed her number. There was no answer. He was feeling concern, A line of four Taxis were parked - beside the depot: he hailed one and directed the driver to the Calloway farm. His mother's car was parked in the shed beside the house. He paid the driver and took his luggage to the porch. The driver left in a rush. Naught stepped up on the porch and knocked. When no one answered he opened the door and went inside. His mother lay groaning in the Kitchen floor, five feet away lay a man in a pool of blood, he checked his pulse and there was none; he was dead. He went back to his mother. He could see that she was laying across a baseball bat. He rolled her body slightly to the left and pulled the bat from beneath her. He went to the bedroom and took a pillow to put beneath her head for she was having trouble breathing. He then ran to the phone and called the sheriff's office and asked them to come and to send an ambulance. It seemed like forever, but fifteen minutes later the sheriff's patrol car pulled into the yard, an ambulance right behind him. Sheriff Halbert Thompson entered the house followed by his deputy, John James.

Ambulance, emergency personnel loaded his mother onto a stretcher, while the Sheriff was checking the dead man for a pulse.

"He's dead," Naught declared

"Did you kill him?"

"No, I didn't kill him, I just got here."

"You know these people?"

"Yes, the lady in the ambulance is my mother."

"I'm guessing the dead man is my father."

"Guessing? Don't you know if it's your own damn father? The lawman asked gruffly."

"Not for certain. I haven't seen him in more than fifteen years. He left my momma, my brother and me when I was seven and I have not seen hide nor hair of him since!"

"Look Sheriff I need to go to be with my mother, I'll answer all your questions at the hospital."

"No, you will ride with me to the hospital, then you will go with us to my office."

"John, sack up that bat. Looks like it could be the weapon that killed the man. See if he's got any identification on him, and we need to tape off the whole house." I'll call the coroner and the State Police; they have a good forensic team I am told. You stay here until I return. Look around the place and report anything peculiar. Shouldn't be more than an hour."

"The lady appeared to be in a coma. If she lives, she may be able to identify the killer. But She's in pretty bad shape, the sheriff added.

The sheriff didn't have to call the state police. They drove up just as they were getting ready to leave. Naught did not recognize the two officers who climbed out of the patrol car.

The two came to the sheriff's car and spoke through the window and looked Naught McCullough over good.

The state policeman stuck out his hand introduced himself. "Gene Edwards," he said, and this my assistant, Miss Angela Livingston, Chief Detective."

"What you got Sheriff?"

"Dead man who looks to be in his fifties. Appears to have been killed with a Louisville slugger baseball bat. Didn't look like but one blow, however. Must have been a strong SOB. John, my deputy will fill you in. Hope you will do the same when you get your report."

"Will do. Have a good day. We should have you a report by day after tomorrow."

The sheriff drove to the hospital on the hill and got there just as the ambulance was dropping Mrs. McCullough at the emergency room entrance. The Sheriff and Naught followed the EMT's into the emergency entrance and second later the doctor and a nurse wheeled her away to an examination room. They took a seat in the emergency waiting room. It was a place set aside where police officers could wait for the doctor to come out and give them a report on the condition of the patient. It was nearly a half hour later before the doctor came out.

"She has taken a pretty bad beating, but she will live. We gave her medicine to help ease the pain, so she may sleep for several hours. You should be able to talk to her in the morning. Naught got up and started for the bank of pay phones that lined the outside of the emergency room.

"Where are you going?" the Sheriff yelled.

"To use the phone. I have to call my brother. He works at the lumber Yard."

"Ok, but make it quick, I have to go pick up my deputy."

"Naught quickly looked up the number for the Webb law firm, dropped in a coin and dialed the number. A lady answered the phone.

"Can I speak to Zack Calloway.? Tell him it's Naught McCullough, It's urgent!"

Seconds later Zack came on the line."

"Hey Naught, what's up? I heard you were coming home for a few days. When can we get together?"

"Right now, if you can. I am at the hospital with my mother. She has been badly beaten. I am with the County Sheriff. Someone killed my father at my mother's house, and it looks like I'm the prime suspect."

"I'll be right there. Don't say a word to that smart assed sheriff. Is there anyone else I need to call for you"?

"Yeah, my brother at the lumber yard, and Penny if you don't mind."

"No problem. Remember don't say anything to the Sheriff."

"Zack knocked on the door of Mr. Webb, and said, Mr. Webb. I need to speak to you."

"Come in. What's going on?"

I have to leave for a while and may not be back this afternoon. My friend Naught McCullough is in a pickle, his mother has been beaten and his father has been killed. Naught thinks the sheriff wants to pin it on him. I have to go, but can you have Mrs. Free call Nate Calloway at the Lumber yard and Penelope Johnson and tell them Naught is at the hospital with his mother, that she has been injured. Penny's number is in the book; Penny Johnson."

"Let me know if I can help, as he waved me out the door.

It took no more than five minutes to drive from downtown Tupelo to the hospital. When I entered the emergency room, I could see the lawman and Naught through the glass windows of the waiting area. Neither of them looked very happy. I didn't wait for an invitation by hospital officials, I just went in like I was supposed to be there.

When I entered the room, I reached for Naught's hand and pulled him to myself and gave my old friend a big hug.

"This your brother?" The sheriff asked.

Penny Johnson

29

Defending Naught McCullough

"No, THIS IS MY good friend Zack Calloway, and my Attorney if I should need one."

"Thought you were calling your brother?"

"Did!" He was out on a delivery."

"The sheriff wants to take me to his office for questioning, Naught said to Zack, but I need to stay with my mother."

"Unless he intends to arrest you, it will not be necessary for you to go to his office tonight. The sheriff is going to look mighty foolish having arrested a decorated Marine with a bronze star to his credit when the investigation is over. He may never be elected again."

"That would be such a shame", Naught panned.

"Alright, Mr. Attorney you have won this round, but I'm sending a deputy over to keep an eye on the suspect until I can get some more answers."

The two old friends watched the sheriff leave the hospital and they went outside to the regular waiting area just outside the ICU.

Naught filled Zack in on what he knew, which was not much. Zack pulled out a little notebook from his jacket pocket and asked a few questions.

"What time did you get to Tupelo, and how did you get here?"

Naught ran through his actions from the time he arrived on the Greyhound bus just after eleven this morning. He had no idea who had killed his father.

Zack made some notes and put the notebook away.

Ten minutes later Joe Webb and Naught's brother came into the waiting just ahead of Penny.

Joe introduced himself to Naught and immediately asked about Mrs. McCullough. Naught went to his brother and hugged him like he was more than just a brother, for Naught had been brother and father to Notch, as his brother called him.

When Penney had her turn at Naught, she welcomed him into her arms and kissed him on the lips. It seemed apparent to me that Penny cared much more for Naught than she had let on when we had talked before. I was alright with that for it seemed I had no time for romance.

Trying to spend plenty of time with my son and getting started at the law firm consumed nearly all my time. I liked Penny more than a little, but it seemed obvious that nothing was going to happen there. Naught seemed to have won Penny's heart.

When Penny was leaving the hospital, however, she came to me and asked if I could come by her house Sunday Morning and talk for a while.

"I'll have to drop my son off at Pappy's. My housekeeper is off on Sundays and she's taking the train to Memphis for some sightseeing. If my parents have other plans, I will have to bring ZI with me."

"That's fine; I would love to meet him. Try to come about ten if you can, I will be staying with Naught at the hospital on Sunday afternoon, "She added.

"Penny said goodbye to everyone and Naught came and sat next to his brother.

I told Naught about my son and explained that I needed to go home and check on him.

"I want to tell you, Zack, that I'm thinking of asking Penny to marry me. I hope you're ok with that."

"Sure, she and I are friends, nothing more. She is a beautiful, sweet lady. I wish you both the best."

I had a sick feeling in my stomach. I liked Penny much more than I was willing to tell Naught. I had apparently lost another woman I cared for.

"I will be back first thing in the morning. However, if the sheriff attempts to arrest you, I will be here in five minutes.

"Try your best to keep them from arresting me. Otherwise, I have to report it to my commanding office. That would not be good for me and my future in the Marines. They are not very forgiving of marines who get in trouble with the law."

"I will talk to Mr. Webb at the law firm and see what we might be able to do to help. He is old friends with the Circuit Judge. I'll see if they can persuade the sheriff to wait until he has seen the coroner's report before he takes any action against you."

The next morning, I had breakfast with ZJ and headed toward the Hospital. Two sheriff patrol cars were parked outside the emergency room. I went in and found that the waiting area outside the ICU was empty. I asked the nurse about Jannie McCullough.

"They moved her out of ICU early this morning into a regular room. First floor, room 124. She is doing very well to have taken such a beating."

I found Naught, his brother, and Joe Webb on the first floor waiting room. The sheriff and a deputy were in serious conversation with Naught. I walked over and asked how Mrs. McCullough was doing.

"Except for the bruises and soreness, she seems fine," Naught replied.

"What is your business, Sheriff? Do you intend to arrest my client?"

"No, I got a call from the Circuit Judge this morning asking me to hold off on that. Wanted me to wait until we get the report from the coroner and the State Police. He said that Gene Edwards, the head investigator had promised he would have his report the first thing in the morning. If he doesn't have the report in his hand by eight in the morning, I am going to arrest your client and hold him on suspicion of murder. I can hold him for forty-eight hours."

I believed what Naught had told me, but, I thought, "If not Naught, then who?" I hoped that the State Police report would shed some light on the case. Naught certainly had motive, but did he have the opportunity, in my opinion the answer was no. The coroner's report should give us that information when he established the time of death.

Sunday morning, I dropped ZJ off with Pappy and Momma. Momma said they were going to drive over to Big Flat, but that they would be happy for their grandson to go along with them. I made it to Penney's just after ten o'clock. She was waiting on the front steps.

She came to the truck and opened the door for me. I stepped down from the truck and she put her arm around me and walked me to the porch swing.

"I'm glad you came. I was afraid you wouldn't after I had kissed Naught at the hospital."

"Yeah, I gave it some thought. Even thought about taking you out to the big pond and drowning you. A lot of things crossed my mind."

"Well, you need not worry about that, it meant nothing: just wanted Naught to feel better."

"Well, it may have meant nothing to you, but it sure meant something to Naught. He's planning on asking you to marry him. He wants to do it while he is on leave."

"Well, she said, that is not going to happen; ever! I would never marry someone who would want to take me away from Tupelo, and Pop."

"When he finds that out, I may have to defend him in *two* murder cases." I panned.

"So where does that leave us?" She asked.

"Not sure. Do you want a relationship, or are you only toying with my fragile affections, like you are with Naught?"

"Well now, that's just not fair," she said, standing up, her hands on her hips. "I wanted a relationship until I learned that you had a son. That changed everything for me. I never thought you would go around sleeping with every woman that came along! What kind of man would have sex with the mother of the girl he professed to love! Answer me that Mr. big shot lawyer?"

Penny had nailed me for the no-good SOB I really was.

"You are right, I deserved that. I don't deserve a girl like you. So, I asked, "where does that leave us. It happened and I can't go back and change anything. And when I look at my son, I realize that I wouldn't want to. If we can't get past that, then I don't reckon there's anything for us. For that I am truly sorry."

I got up and started for my truck. Penny called after me.

"Wait," she said. She walked up to me and put her hand on my shoulder. "There's something I want to tell you."

"There's only one girl I know that would forgive you for anything you did and would love you without reservation.

"My mother is already taken, I laughed.

"Not your Mother Zack, Charlie," she yelled. "She loves you no matter what. She is a grown woman now. Don't screw up that kind of love Zack!"

Penny turned and walked back to the house. I stood there stunned. I then turned and got in my truck and drove away. Thoughts of Charlie loving me so clouded my mind. She must have been devastated when she learned what had happened between me and Marie.

THE CORONERS REPORT

I was waiting at the sheriff's office when Gene Edwards delivered his report to the Lawman. He had a copy of the file for me too. I took it and scanned it quickly.

"The coroner's report, Edwards said, concluded that Naught's Daddy had died of blunt force trauma to the head, but was not caused by a baseball bat. There were fingerprints on the bat of at least three people, one of which were those of Sergeant McCullough. We have not yet identified who the other prints belong to. We have the FBI running their files. Forensic didn't find much else, but we found tiny cinders near the dead man but no clues as to how they got there, or how long they have been there. But it is unusual to find cinders inside the house. We also found blood on the corner of the cookstove which matches the blood type of the deceased. The team believes that when the man was hit with the baseball bat, he may have pitched forward and hit his head when he was falling."

"So you're saying that the blow from the bat did not kill the deceased." I stated.

"It appears so. There is clearly a bruised mark across the man's back and shoulder that matches up with the bat."

"It appears to us, that whoever hit the deceased man with the bat, didn't intend to kill him. He was most likely just trying to stop the attack on Mrs. McCullough. That is speculation, of course, but it makes sense," Edwards said. "We are not finished with our investigation. We need to find the person who did this, if it wasn't Sergeant McCullough, we need to talk with Mrs. McCullough to see if she knew who did it or has any ideas about who might have come to her rescue. The coroner also found that the dead man had a high alcohol level in his blood. He was probably very drunk."

I said nothing, but one person was running through my mind. *Lucas!* I asked the sheriff if he intended to file charges against my client.

"No, he said the coroner set the time of death at between nine and eleven. I know that Sergeant McCullough didn't get off the bus until after eleven and didn't get his cab to the farm until after eleven thirty. Your client is free to go."

I told Naught that I had to run an errand and would see him later in the day. I went to my truck and headed to the farm.

Ten minutes later I pulled up to the big barn and got out. I expected to find Lucas pounding on his anvil, but he was nowhere to be found. Lucas had bought himself an old flatbed truck last week, but there was no sign of the truck. I walked to the blacksmith shop and was shocked to find that there were no tools or equipment anywhere, not even a horseshoe. I then went to the room that we had made into living quarters, it was as if the whole place had never been lived in. Only the cot that he slept and two ladderback chairs and a small table were the only items in the room. Lucas had loaded up his entire life and took to the wind it appeared. As I was leaving, I found a note nailed to the back of the door at the entrance to his hovel.

Zack.

"I hit the man with the bat, but I didn't mean to kill him. I thought he was going to kill Mrs. Mac. Don't try to find me, you will not be able to. I was sent to you for a purpose, and my job is done. Tell Charlie I love her.

Lucas

I left the note nailed on the door and didn't touch anything. I figured the sheriff was going to want to talk to Lucas, but I doubted he ever would. I knew Charlie would want to see Lucas, and she would leave no stone unturned. Naught was in the clear and Mrs. McCullough was recovering nicely. I had done my job as his attorney and as his friend, but there were still clouds on Naught's horizon. He loved Penny and would be devastated when he found out that she didn't really love him and had no intention of marriage. That storm too would pass in time. But it would do damage and leave scars that might take years to heal. Scars of war Naught had borne, but scars that a Penny would leave could be longer lasting.

Zack and ZJ (on horseback)

*"PROBLEM? YOU'VE GOT TO NIP IT IN THE BUD
ANDY. NIP IT, NIP IT, RIGHT IN THE BUD"*

Don Knots/ The Andy Griffith Show

30

Lucas in the Wind

I WONDERED WHAT LUCAS meant when he said he was sent to us for a purpose. Sent by whom? And I also wondered where he would go. Since he took all his blacksmith tools it seemed obvious to me that he would set up shop somewhere. He had told us that he had come from Rock Hill, a little community ten or twelve miles from Tupelo. Perhaps I could find a clue there. He also had a brother in Memphis. The State Police and the sheriff would want that information. They would also want to see the note that Lucas had left on the door. I wondered too, why he would run away when he knew he was only trying to save Jannie McCullough. A lot of questions needed to be answered. I was sure Gene Edwards would get to the bottom of it if anybody could.

I spent the rest of the afternoon making calls. I knew that Lucas had bought his truck from the Chevrolet dealership in Tupelo. I talked with the salesperson, Jack Dirksen, and asked if he remembered Lucas.

"Yes, I remembered him, he paid four hundred dollars cash. I don't think he had driven very much, for he had a heck of a time just getting out of the parking lot. Dang near run over old man Hatcher, who runs the barber shop over on Broadway. He was hobbling along on his cane and Mr. Lucas was grinding gears and headed straight for the old man. Hatcher threw down that cane and ran for his life, cursing every breath. I wondered if he even had a driver's license."

Friday, I had heard nothing more from law enforcement and I decided to take a drive over to Rock Hill to see if anyone in the little community could help me. I called Mr. Webb and asked if he knew anyone there. I needed to find Lucas before the sheriff got his hands on him and threw him in jail.

"It's a one store, one street, town. JP Clark has run that store for fifty years. If anyone could help it would be him. Stop by and have yourself a Coke and a pack of peanuts and he'll give you a hundred dollars' worth of information for your fifteen cents."

I went by and picked up ZJ to ride along with me and I saw Charlie and ZJ walking down the sidewalk. Charlie carrying a large grocery sack in one arm and holding ZJ's hand in the other. I stopped right behind them and honked. They both jumped and turned, then laughed. They climbed in beside me, ZJ yelled "Shotgun!" That meant he wanted the window seat.

"Oh shoot, Charlie feinted disappointment, you beat me again."

"What's in the sack?"

"Groceries. Doing some shopping for your maid."

"Housekeeper," I corrected.

"More like a servant."

''You're mean," I said, and poked her with my elbow

"And you are a knuckle head," she said, poking me back.

"I'm going to make a run over to Rock Hill, and you two can ride along if you want to. You have to tell Miss Beverly. Tell her we will be back in time for supper."

"I'm sure she will be tickled about that,'' Charlie said sarcastically. "You could take us out to eat."

"Are You paying?" I asked.

"With what?"

"Ok, tell Beverly we are going out to eat. We will go to the diner downtown," I caved. Twenty minutes later I turned off the main highway onto a gravel street and a homemade sign that announced

"Rock Hill. Population 102."

"They must count hogs and chickens," Charlie allowed.

"Not much to it, that's for sure," I said.

I passed a small church house and a few unpainted houses before I saw the Gulf Oil sign that was a landmark for Clark's Store. It was a run-down old building that looked more like an outbuilding than a grocery store. There was a portico that covered two ancient gas pumps and a kerosene drum. The floor under the portico was dirt and sixty years of soda pop bottle tops were buried in the rock-hard soil.

"Well, we're here, I said, come on in and I'll buy you a coke and peanuts."

"Is it safe, Charlie asked."

"It just survived a tornado," I assured her.

"Are you sure it survived?"

We parked the truck and went through a screen door that advertised Camel Cigarettes. The cold drink box was just inside the front door Charlie fished out a root beer from the cold water and ZJ picked a sunspot orange. I took a Coke. A grey-haired old man stood behind the counter. The store was dark and had the strong smell of tobacco, and God only knows what else.

"Howdy folks, can I help you find anything?"

"Peanuts? I asked.

"Sure thing, how many?"

"Three," I nodded, and three drinks.

"Forty-five cents, he said.

I introduced myself and Charlie and ZJ.

"That your wife?" he asked.

That question took me by surprised.

"Not yet," I stammered.

Charlie turned red and walked out of the store. ZJ followed.

"Do you happen to know a fellow by the name of Lucas Robbins that used to have a blacksmith somewhere around here?" I asked.

"Nope. Never has been a blacksmith shop around here anywhere. No Lucas Robbins either. I read the notice that ran in the paper a few years ago. I thought it was a joke."

"You sure about this?" I asked.

"Son I have lived here for seventy years. I know every sole that lives here or has ever lived here. There has never been a Lucas Robbins that lived anywhere near this place."

"Well, I thank you for your help."

"That will be six cents if you are taking the bottles."

I flipped him a dime and said, "keep the change."

He threw up his hand as a goodbye. I walked out shaking my head. It had all been a lie by Lucas, but why?

I walked back to the truck and slid in beside ZJ. Charlie had taken the window seat. She wouldn't even look at me. I made no comment. Minutes later ZJ had his head in Charlie's lap. By the time we were back on the main highway he was sleeping peacefully.

When we got back to town it was near suppertime, so we went inside to freshen up and I changed from my suit into jeans and a Tee shirt.

After we finished with our meal. I drove back to the house, and I tucked ZJ into bed. Charlie said that she needed to go home, that Momma would be worried. I told her that I would drive her.

"No thanks, she said, I'd rather walk"

"Then I will walk with you. We need to talk."

"What do we have to talk about? Charlie asked."

"Well, to begin with, I need to tell you about Lucas."

"Secondly, I want to know why you always seem to be angry with me about something."

Charlie grabbed her purse and went out the door. I followed. She was walking fast, and I had to run to catch up. When I caught up with her, I grabbed her shoulder and spun her around. She was red faced and angry.

"WHAT!" she yelled, "say what you want to say and leave me alone."

"Lucas is missing," I said. "He apparently took everything he owned with him."

"Missing, do you mean that he is gone?"

"Yes, and I don't have a clue where he might be."

I explained what had happened to Mrs. McCullough and the note Lucas had left. She looked stunned.

"Where would he go? She asked"

"I don't know. That is why I went to Rock Hill, he had told us that he once had a blacksmith shop there, but it was all a lie. He never lived there. I don't know what else he told us that was also a lie. Maybe everything. I need to find him before the sheriff does. He may charge him with murder. Do you have any ideas?" I asked.

"None, he never told me much about himself. It was always about learning, and of course that was years ago. We haven't talked much since then. I would never have thought he would leave without telling me goodbye."

"Yeah, I know, he was crazy about you," I agreed.

"Well, at least there was one man who really cared about me, she said sarcastically."

"You know damn well how much I care about you, damnit!"

"Yes, I know, you love me and treat me like a sister. Well, l I'm not your damn sister and I just want to be treated like a woman; a woman that loves you with all her heart, and if I seem angry at you, it's with good cause. You made love to my best friend's mother, for Christ's sake! It was your own sweetheart's mother. Do you have no shame at all? It broke my heart to know that you did such a thing. I cried for a week when I found out."

I had no response to that for it was all true and I knew it. Penny had been right too, but that was water under the bridge. I have a son that I love dearly, and I couldn't go back and change a thing.

"If you can't see that I am no longer a little girl, but a full-grown woman, then I want nothing more to do with you. Just go on poking every woman that comes along and see where that gets you. It will make you a lonely old man, some day, she cried."

She broke loose from my grip and ran away from me. I was sick to my stomach watching her go. I wondered if this storm would ever pass. Love, I was reminded, was never black and white, but many shades of grey. My relationship with Charlie was definitely in the grey area, and I didn't know if I could fix it.

I spent most of the weekend on the farm, teaching ZJ to ride the black mare. He took to it right off and was riding beside me before we stopped for lunch. I had made sandwiches for lunch, and we sat at the little table in room made for Lucas."

"I wish Charlie was here," ZJ said, "I like her a lot, and I bet she would like to ride and picnic with us."

"Well, I'm not so sure, she is not happy with me right now.'"

"Why? He asked.

"Oh, it's a grown-up problems," I shrugged.

"Don't be mad at her," he said. "It's probably just a woman thing. That's what pappy says when Momma Callahan gets angry at him about something."

"Yeah, that's sounds like Pappy alright," I laughed.

Sunday morning ZJ and I went to the hospital to see Mrs. McCullough. Momma and Pappy were there with Joe Webb. Mrs. McCullough was sitting up in bed and was ready to go home. She still had large bruises on her face and arms. She said Naught had just left to go and see Penny. I wondered if he has popped the question. I knew he had already bought a ring. I stayed for a few minutes and left with ZJ. I wanted to see Charlie before Momma and Pappy got home. I was at the door when Joe stopped and called after me. I was just outside the door but continued to walk down the hall.

"What about the divorce papers we filed?" He asked.

"Can't divorce a dead man," I grinned. You are free to marry Jannie, anytime, if she still wants you. She's probably backed out by now, I laughed. You didn't kill him, did you?".

"Hell no, but I probably would have if I would have been there. Any man who would beat a woman like that deserves to be killed."

"Probably a good thing you were with Pappy at the sale barn when it happened. When are you two having the wedding?"

"Soon. Before Naught's leave is over. He's here for two weeks before he leaves for California."

"Let me know the date," I said as I was walking away. You must have put a hex on that woman to get her to marry you," I laughed.

"Shoot, that woman is getting a bargain; the cream of the crop."

"More like getting soured buttermilk," I laughed again.

I drove to Momma's and Pappy's place, hoping I would catch Charlie a home. ZJ ran to the porch and banged on the door. Robert and Charlie came out.

"ZJ, why don't you and Robert go and shoot some baskets. I need to talk to Charlie alone."

Robert frowned, and rolled his eyes, he apparently felt he was too good to be playing with a five-year-old, but he went inside and retrieved the basketball. I asked Charlie to sit with me in the swing.

"More talk, huh? Charlie said. How are you going to hurt my feeling this time? Why don't you just shoot me and put me out of my misery for good?"

Charlie Calloway and Zack Calloway

DON'T BE CRUEL TO A HEART THAT'S TRUE, I DON'T WANT NO OTHER LOVE. ALL I WANT IS YOU,

Elvis Presley "Don't Be Cruel"

31

Heart to Heart with Charlie

I LOOKED HER STRAIGHT in those sea-blue eyes, and said, "Charlie, I never want to hurt you again. I have loved you since the day you came to live with us, nearly nine years ago, but not the same way a man loves a woman. For six years I thought of you as my sister. Now you are almost nineteen, and a beautiful woman who was never my sister. I will admit I went off the rails for a while and I know now how much that must have hurt you, I can't go back and change that. What's done is done. It's been hard for me to get used to not being your big brother. I am not a womanizer like you seem to think I am. If you give me a chance, I will show you that."

She was silent for a moment. She turned her head away and looked off into the distance. When she turned, she looked me in the eyes. "What I want is for someone to love me like my daddy loved my momma, and the way Pappy loves your mother. I want settle for anything less; And I won't give anything less in return. If you can do that, we have a chance. If you can't, we have nothing else to discuss."

"Ride out to the farm with me this afternoon There's something I want to show you. You could fix us a picnic lunch if you wanted," I suggested.

"Don't push your luck, Buster," she said.

"Ok, I'll pack the lunch."

"No thanks, I'll do it. You buy the drinks."

"No problem, Pappy keeps drinks at the farm on ice; saves me a dime."

I got up when Momma and Pappy drove up. I waited until they were on the porch.

"What are you two up to?" Pappy asked.

"Planning for a picnic. I going to take Charlie out to where I plan on building my home."

"House, Pappy corrected. You don't build a home, you make it. It takes more than one person to make a home, and it is hard work. You can have a three-story mansion and still not have a home. Two people can live in a two-room shanty and have a family of five and have a wonderful home. Home is never about a house."

"I get that Pappy, but I want to give the ones I love a nice place to live."

"Nothing wrong with that as long as you can afford it,"

Pappy Said.

"A very wise woman told me not to spoil my son with things, but to teach him. Teach him how to make it on his own, and to use my money to help others, and that's what I aim to do. I can make a good living practicing Law; I don't need a big bank account."

"Well, he said, maybe you can do something about these people who are about to lose their jobs," handing me yesterday's paper, and pointing to the front-page headline.

> *"Highway 6 Lumber and Supply is closing. A hundred or more employees are to be laid off in one week. A company spokesman said the owners are also closing the West Point and Columbus operations as well. The spokesman, who asked not to be identified, said the company had been losing money for three years, and they had no choice but to cease operations. The spokesman said that the owners had sought a buyer for the business. but had no reasonable offers. The spokesman said that all employees would receive one-week wages*

as severance pay. The company plans an auction on the inventory and real property in the near future. The spokesman apologized for the inconvenience, and the for the loss of jobs to the city.

I couldn't believe what I was reading. Pappy and Wayne Purnell had made the Purnell lumber and Supply into a thriving and highly profitable operation, and then doing the same with stores in Columbus and West Point. There were other small lumber suppliers but nothing like Purnell's Lumber. Builders and contractors needed the big lumber company for Tupelo was a growing, thriving, town. I have an idea, and I will talk to you about it a little later. But was wondering if you could look out after ZJ while I take Charlie riding out at the farm."

"Sure, Charlie loves to ride the horses and she sometimes helps me put out hay for the cows. She just about has them all named. I love to hear her talk to them."

"We'll be home before dark, so don't worry, I assured Pappy."

"I'm not worried about Charlie, I worry about you," Pappy offered. "Don't you dare hurt that girl," he warned.

"I wouldn't do that, that much I promise you," I said. I wondered, however. if Pappy knew Charlie's true feelings for me. Probably not. If he did, he probably wouldn't let her near me.

Charlie was making us a lunch, and I went out and shot baskets with Robert and ZJ while I waited for her to finish. When she came out, she carried a tote bag and wore white shorts with a black blouse, tied at the waist. She was quite a woman.

We drove to the big barn and saddled the mare and the Dapple Grey. I picked up some drinks from Pappy's cooler and then we rode out toward the ridge where I had been kissed by Penny Johnson. We crossed the shallow shoals with the horses and dismounted beneath the big White Oak. Charlie had brought a blanket and she spread it beneath the tree. We sat down and leaned back against the massive oak and just marveled at the beauty of the place.

"Pappy gave me and Willy each five hundred acres when we finished college, and I am going to build my house right here on this ridge. I want ZJ to learn about farming, cattle, and horses and how to make his way in the world. I want a wife who will help me do that for him and our other children.

"You have other children?" Charlie smiled.

"No, of course not, but I want more," I said.

"Do you have someone in mind to help you?"

"Yes, as a matter of fact, I do", I answered.

"Momma and Pappy will probably disown both of us, but I want you to be my wife, Charlie."

32

The Proposal

"YOU DO, DO YOU?" Charlie grinned, "I guess I'll have to think on it. You have never even kissed me. Like Pappy says, you should always sleep on important decision like that. I'll let you know in a day or two."

"Well, you better not wait too long. You know what a womanizer I am," I laughed. "Would you be willing to allow me a kiss while you are thinking?"

"I think that would be allowable, while I'm thinking on it."

We embraced, and kissed, there on the spot where I wanted to make my home. It was long and sweet. I was hungry for her love and so was she, but she pushed me away.

"That's enough for me to think on," she said.

"There's more I have to tell you before we go," I told her.

"You're already married, I suppose," Charlie grinned.

"No this is no joke, but in the interest of full disclosure, there is something I want to tell you. It's more that you may have to think on."

"Ok, let's hear it," she said.

"I am very rich," I stuttered.

"Rich?" she laughed. "You just told me your father gave you this land. So, I know you are rich in my eyes."

"No, I am really rich. Like millions rich."

"Where would you get millions.",

"That is what I want you to know about. It came from Marie. She got it in an law suit settlement and she wanted me to promise her that I would not spoil ZJ with buying things, she wanted me to use some of the money to help people, and I have an Idea on how I'm going to use some of it I am going to keep enough to give our children a good education and I want to add to this farm, for their inheritance. I don't need a lot of money to be happy, when people around me are needing help. I am thinking of making an offer on the lumber company. If they close it down, nearly a hundred people in Tupelo will lose their jobs. I don't want that to happen. A lot of them are my friends. What do you think, Charlie?

"I think it's a great idea, but how are you going to run the lumber yard and be a lawyer too?"

"I've got the makings of a plan in my mind, and I have to talk to Pappy and some other folks for some help. I will also have to talk with the current owners. Pappy and Bonnie Little will know what the business is worth, and they may want to invest in the business as well. Jannie McCullough will know about the inventory at the Tupelo store, but Pappy will have to look at the Columbus location and West Point locations. I want your approval before I start the process, because I want your help. It's another thing you have to sleep on."

"You know that you have my approval, how I can help."

"I will explain later but there is plenty you can do. Right now, though, we must go. Pappy will be coming to see if I am behaving myself with you." We rode down to the widest place in the creek, dismounted, took off our shoes, and waded across in ankle deep, ice-cold water.

Twenty minutes later we were in Pappy's front yard. Momma in the big rocker and ZJ asleep in her arms. Pappy came out the front door with a glass of iced tea in his hand as we were walking up. Charlie was holding my arm. He stopped, looked at me and then at Charlie and shook his head and said, "well I'll be damned." He then sat in the rocker next to Momma, nodding for us to take the swing.

"I know that you two have something to tell us, but you better make it quick, Naught McCullough is in the city Jail, and he called for you."

"What to heck has he done?"

"Drunk and disorderly, and he pushed the Johnson girl around some, but she hasn't filed charges yet, but he wants to see you."

"Well, he is just going to have to wait. What Charlie and I have to say is far more important. I was nervous, so I just came out with it. "I have asked Charlie to be my wife."

I thought Momma was going to drop ZJ.

"WHAT! asked her to be your wife? She's your sister, for heaven's Sake."

"No, Mom, she is not, and never has been. I have asked her, but she hasn't given me an answer yet. We are going to build a house, if she says yes, on the land that Pappy gave us, and that's where we will make our home!"

"Tears came to Momma's eyes as she shook her head. She is only eighteen, she's just a child."

"No Momma Callahan, I am not a child. I am a woman, and I am in love with your son. I love him like you love Pappy, Charlie said firmly. Do you remember how you loved Pappy when you were sixteen? That is when you married him."

"Well, of course I do," she said with a slight grin as she looked at Pappy.

Pappy turned red and squirmed.

"Well, that's the same way I feel about Zack. I know he has flaws, he has made mistakes, as we all do, but I know he loves me. He has proved that to me time and time again. Please don't be angry at us; be happy for us."

"We are not angry at you," Pappy said, "we are just worried about our children. Sounds like you both have your minds made. I hope you are as happy as Allie and I have been, and you both have added to that for us."

"Pappy, can I borrow your truck for a little while?"

"What's wrong with yours? You are taking my daughter, and now you want my truck You are pushing your luck," he grinned.

"Nothing, I want Charlie to go and see about Penny. Her truck is in the shop getting a new clutch. If Naught has hurt that girl, I may use the Louisville Slugger on him again. While Charlie does that, I'm going to the jail to see what all they have charged him with and see if I can get him out."

"Sure," Pappy said "go on and do your Lawyering business. We'll talk more when you two get back."

I kissed Charlie and drove to the four-cell jail located in the basement of City Hall. I knew just about everyone in City Hall. Many were former classmates and the rest I knew from working at the law firm. Willy Franks welcomed me and filled me in on what had happened and then led me back to the cell where Naught was stretched out on a cot that was chained to the wall. Naught stood up when I neared the door.

"Well, you took your own sweet time getting here", he said as Franks opened the cell door.

"Started not to come at all. I don't have much use for men who mistreat women. Your Mother taught you better; that much I know. And when did you take up drinking?"

"First time I ever took a drink, and I don't know why I got so angry when Penny turned down my marriage proposal."

"Well, so far, they have only charged you with being drunk and disorderly. If Penny files charges for battery, you could be looking at jail time. I can't believe you hit that girl. I sent Charlie over to talk to her and find out what her intentions are. Do you have bail money, I asked?"

"Depends, he said. How much is this going to cost me?"

"The judge will decide that I said.

"Can you get me out?"

"I'll have to wait until I talk to Charlie, but if I do, you are not to go anywhere near Penny Johnson. It would be best if you got on the first bus leaving town, but I know your Momma is planning on you being at the wedding. Which will likely be toward the end of your leave time. We have been good friends for a long time, I said, but if you ever lay your hands on another woman in anger again, don't call me."

"I hear you: I wasn't expecting to get dressed down by my own, damn lawyer."

"Well, you needed it," I said as I turned to leave.

I called for the jailer to let me out and asked what Judge would be overseeing the case."

"Henry Keeler, he said, and he conducts most of his misdemeanor cases over the phone. He is eighty-five years old, and he don't drive anymore. He is my uncle, you know. I will call him and see what he wants to do, if you would like."

"Yeah, that would be great. Franks left me in the small waiting area and went to make a call. While he was gone, Charlie called to tell me that Penny was not filing any charges against Naught, and that Penny was fine except for a black eye and a sore butt, when she fell after he hit her. Franks returned in ten minutes, carrying a clip board.

"Keeler said for me to fine the boy a hundred dollars and a day in jail, which he has already served. Sign these forms, cough up a hundred dollars, and your client is free to go,"

I waited until the officer retrieved my client.

Judge Keeler has fined you a hundred dollars. Do you have that much on you, I asked."

"Yeah, I can manage that."

"My fee is also a hundred dollars. I would normally only charge fifty, but the extra is for ruining my Sunday with perhaps the most beautiful woman in Tupelo and my future wife."

"Wife? I figured you would never marry. Who is the unfortunate woman?"

"Charlie." I grinned.

"YOUR SISTER? I thought there were laws against such things, He said loudly.

"Well, as it turns out, she is not even related to me. I'll tell you about it later. Can I give you a lift to somewhere? I asked. Where are you staying?"

"With Mom and Notch. You mind dropping me off?"

"No, it's fine. Come on, let's go. I'm driving Pappy's truck, and he'll be walking the floor if I am gone too long."

When we got to the farm, Mrs. McCullough and Joe Webb were sitting in the porch swing and Notch was working on an old lawn mower. Notch was a natural mechanic and could fix just about anything mechanical. I waved out the window to them, let Naught out and headed for home. It had been a busy day and I couldn't wait to see Charlie.

When I got back to the house, Pappy was waiting. He was sitting in the rocker trying to get Squat to drink a liquid from a coffee cup. A bottle of bourbon sitting beside him. Squat was not being cooperative. Don't reckon Squat liked the taste of good whiskey.

"What are you doing Pappy, trying to get Squat drunk?

"Nope, he's been feeling poorly, lately. Can't hardly get up and down anymore. Won't eat. The Vet said he has arthritis really bad. And there is not much he could do for him. Doctor Little told me to crush three aspirin in a little whiskey. He said it would help ease the pain." Little said he's on his last leg. He asked me If I didn't want him to put to sleep. It was about all I could do. I told Little; I'd have *him* put to sleep before I would Squat. He's been a fine dog and mighty good company over the years, and I aim to let him die of natural causes.

Pappy, there's something I want to talk to you about, I want to talk with miss Bonnie and Joe Webb too. Can you get them to come over here tonight for an hour or so?

I guess so, I don't know. I can call them and see.

"It's important, I said.

Pappy got Squat to drink the whiskey he had in the cup and offered him a little more. To my surprise Squat drank it and looked at Pappy like he wanted more.

"You have done made a drunk out of your best friend I panned."

"Naw, Squat can hold his liquor," Pappy replied.

33

Saving A Company

At seven o'clock all the folks that I had asked Pappy to contact were seated around the big table in Pappy's dining room. I sat at the head of the table with Charlie to my left and Momma and Pappy to my right, Joe and Jannie, Bonnie and Doctor Little took up the remaining chairs. I had hoped Will would come, but military duties prevented it.

Momma had made fried apple turnovers and coffee for a dessert. When all had been served, I told the group that I had asked Pappy to call them for a specific purpose. I then handed each person a copy of the newspaper article that announced the closing of the Lumber and supply company.

"I was shocked when I read the article, I said. The Lumber company has been a vital part of this community for many years. It has provided over a hundred good paying jobs to our friends and neighbors. The company has been the main supplier to dozens of builders and contractors.

I have recently inherited a very large sum of money who asked me in her last will, to use the money as I saw fit, but it was this person's wish that a good portion of the funds be used to help those in need.

"What are you suggesting Zack, that we establish a fund to help the people who will lose their jobs.

"No, that would just be a temporary fix, I'm suggesting that the people in this room make an offer to buy the Lumber Company and keep it open.

That took everyone's eyes away from the dessert, before them and on me.

"That will take a chunk of change, son. And a lot of business expertise, Pappy offered.

"Yes, and we are not close to being ready to make an offer. That is why I have asked this group to participate. We have in this room all the expertise, and capital needed to make an offer. Joe has the knowledge of how big business is financed if needed.

Jannie, here knows the current inventory, of the business. Bonnie, Momma and Pappy have knowledge of the whole works and can access what needs to be done to make the business profitable again. If the group wants me to pursue this matter, I will be happy to do so. If not, we just let the matter drop. Willy and I both I both grew up in the business and can also offer input, but for now I just need to know whether to contact the current owners for discussion.

I took a vote and everyone voted to have me contact the current owners, to make arrangements to have an inventory audit of the business and a look at their profit and loss statements as well as tax filings.

Meanwhile, I had a job, that I liked very much, and a son that also needed my time; And there was Charlie that I wanted to spend time with. It seemed the faster I ran, the farther behind I lagged. The Law firm was growing by leaps and bounds, and we often turned down new clients because there was not enough of us to go around. Mr. Webb had also assigned me the job of recruiting another attorney for the firm. On top of all that was going on in my life Charlie had made me promise to do everything I could to find Lucas. A lot did not add up concerning his disappearance, so I called the two detectives that were already working the case, thinking that they might be able to help. They were in my office at seven the next morning. I poured them coffee and we sat in a semi-circle in front of my desk.

"DOWN EVERY ROAD, THERE'S ALWAYS ONE MORE CITY, I'M ON THE RUN, THE HIGHWAY IS MY HOME."

Merle Haggard, "Lonesome fugitive."

34

Learning About Lucas

"YOU TWO ARE THE only hope I have, it seems, of locating Lucas. I have no leads to follow and no time to follow them if I did. Any ideas, I asked?"

"Well, to tell the truth, we have been on the case from the beginning and have learned a lot about Lucas. Angela's connection with the FBI she learned that Lucas had been in the witness protection program for the past fifteen years. The program trained him as a blacksmith and set him up in business in a small town in East Texas. According to what we could learn from the bureau; he was a witness to mob murders near New Orleans in the late forties. The bureau has moved him several times during the years, but apparently, he felt attention would be brought to him, because of the McCullough incident, so he went on his own way. Unfortunately, that was a big mistake. The mob had eyes on him before he was out of the state of Mississippi. Lucas, I am sorry to have to tell you, was killed twenty miles North of Lafayette, Louisiana yesterday."

That shocked me to the point I was sick at my stomach.

"The bureau thinks he was headed for the swamps. That is where he grew up: near New Iberia, and apparently felt that was where he could lose himself. The only positive thing to come out of this was that there were witnesses to the killing and the bureau have his assassins in custody, and they are apparently talking plenty. I asked the bureau to contact you, since your family was the closest thing to a real family he ever had. I Thought you might want to have some input on his funeral arrangements, and burial, and take control of what few possessions he had. The bureau will deliver the old truck and all his tools and other things as soon as they are finished with the investigation."

Detective Angela Winston said that she was sorry that the State Police had let Lucas slip through their hands.

"What did Lucas mean when he said he was sent to us. Who sent him, and why?"

"The Bureau had eyes on you for two years as a prospective recruit, they probably figured you for an easy mark when it came to helping folks in trouble. They know just about everything there is to know about you and the people you associate with, where you hang out and what you do with your spare time, it must have worked well picking you and your family for a mark." Angela said.

"Where will he be buried; Any Idea?"

"I don't know, but most likely somewhere near where he was raised. The bureau is trying to locate persons who might have known him as a youngster. Otherwise, the Bureau has its places, I can assure you. Most likely the body will be cremated. If I learn anything more, I will let you know."

When the two detectives had left the office, I called Pappy and asked him and Momma to break the news to Charlie. However, she had left for Oxford to register for Fall classes. I was glad, for I thought it best that I break the news to her. It would be painful for her, for I knew she loved Lucas and he loved her. But this too would pass, and the wounds would eventually heal.

I was not wrong about Charlie being extremely upset. She cried for hours after I broke the news to her.

"Will there be a funeral? She asked. Can we go if there is?"

"I can't answer those questions at this time, but I don't think it would be a good idea for any of us to attend a funeral. Those who wanted Lucas killed may be watching and want to harm anyone that he was associated with."

The office was filled with clients the rest of that day and I was bushed after dealing with the Lucas matter. Beverly had a nice dinner prepared for me and ZJ when I finally made it home. Charlie came over and had dinner with us and after dinner we engaged in a game of Uno which made ZJ happy and relieved some of the tension Charlie and I were feeling. We laughed a lot, all of us sitting on the floor in a circle. It was fun, it was almost like having my own family. The joy, however, was not to last, after ZJ and I walked Charlie home and I had tucked ZJ in for the night, Beverly told me she had made a decision, and that she would be returning to Seattle the first of September. I pleaded for her to stay, but to no avail. I offered more money, but that was not the issue. Marie had left her 300,000 dollars from a life insurance policy, and with what she had been able to save, she felt that she could buy a small house and draw a monthly stipend for as long as she lived, she said she might even get a car and learn to drive.

I understood when she explained that she wanted to get on with her own life and hopefully find someone to share it with. She had enough money to live comfortably. There was nothing I could say that would matter. ZJ was going to really miss her, and so would I but the dye was cast, and I would just have to find another housekeeper.

"What are you going to do, Zack?" Charlie asked when I told her that Beverly would be leaving in September."

"Got to find a housekeeper who is young, beautiful, smart enough to teach ZJ, is a good cook, and won't sass me, I grinned."

"Nationwide search, huh? Not likely to find anyone like that in Mississippi. Charlie grinned."

"I know. Going to be hard to find a replacement like Beverly. You have any Ideas?"

"Well, I might. Let me sleep on it, she said"

"Charlie came into my arms, and we kissed. "What a beautiful woman she was."

"What did you decide on our first proposition? Are you going to marry me or not?'

"Yep, I've been sleeping on it for eight years. I made my mind up about you years ago, it just took you a while to come around to my way of thinking. Now we've got to make plans for a wedding. I don't want a big blowout, just family and friends."

"I like the sound of that," I said.

"I have to talk to Momma Calloway. I'm sure she will want to help. We also have to set a date."

"How about tomorrow," I panned.

"Can't. We have to have a license and make reservations for our honeymoon."

"Honeymoon? That sounds like it's going to cost me money."

"You bet it is, but I aim to make it a bargain for what you get in return."

"Well, don't forget I have a job."

"Don't worry, a weekend honeymoon will be all you need, she grinned and did that thing with her eyes."

"We'll see," I said.

*AIN'T NOTHING IN THIS WHOLE WORLD
WORTH A SOLITARY DIME, 'CEPT OLD DOGS
AND CHILDREN AND WATERMELON WINE.*

Tom T. Hall

35

Squat is Feeling Poorly

GETS AN INFUSION

PAPPY HAS BEEN FEEDING Squat a combination of crushed aspirin and Kentucky bourbon whiskey to help with the pain of his arthritis. It seemed to help some, but Squat was acting a little peculiar at times so Pappy had to cut back on the bourbon. Momma said he had taken to howling at the moon. Momma had made him a straw mattress that she placed near the front door, for Pappy had boarded up his Lair beneath the house, He was having trouble crawling out at times and Robert had to crawl under the house to help him. Squat liked his new digs by the door, for he could greet everyone that came in.

Joe Webb told Pappy that he didn't think there was much wrong with Squat. That he was only about ten years old. Pappy said more like twelve, but we did not really know.

Joe said Pappy had spoiled the old dog until he wasn't worth shooting. Joe said all that Squat needed was a little transfusion of female companionship, and the old dog might be plumb cured of arthritis.

"Probably kill him," Pappy lamented.

Pappy decided it was worth a try, however, and decided to allow Squat a romp with a female companion. His cousin, Raymond Calloway in Big Flat had a female Red Tick that was in heat and need an infusion, as he called it. Pappy and Momma and Robert Lewis loaded Squat in the pickup on a Saturday morning and headed for Big Flat, with Squat looking very much like he was on his last leg. Raymond had the big female hound in a pen out behind his barn to keep her away from Curs. When they drove into the yard, Squat raised his head and sniffed the wind. His ears went straight up and his tail straight out. He bailed out of the truck like he'd been shot with rock salt. Through Raymond's chicken yard he ran, Roosters and hen's running, flying, and squawking for dear life. Seconds later he was climbing the fence to get to the Red Tick lady hound. Today, however. She was not such a lady. Squat pranced around that dog pen with his head and tail held high like he was king of the jungle. Didn't seem to have an ounce of arthritis in his bones.

Pappy left Squat with Raymond until Monday, but Squat wasn't ready to leave when Pappy went to pick him up. Pappy had to put a rope on him and drag him to the truck, with him howling like a Lobo every step of the way. Squat had been cured of his arthritis like Joe Webb had said. But he wasn't cured of the big Blue Tick. The next morning Squat was not in his bed when Pappy went to feed him. He called Joe to ask him if he had showed up out at the farm.

Joe said he had not seen him, that he might check the greyhound station, that he was probably on his way to Big Flat. Joe was right, Pappy caught up to him just past the Shiloh Church. He was over half the way to Big Flat. He was loping along like a three-year-old Pup. Pappy had picked up Joe to ride along with him, and they had a mighty hard time coercing Squat to get in the truck. Pappy had brought along the bottle of bourbon, however and he poured Squat a generous bowl full. When he finished drinking, he gave them no more trouble getting into the truck.

Joe told Pappy that he might as well take Squat on to Big Flat and leave him until he had had enough of the Blue Tick. He would wake up one morning, look at the Blue Tick, remember the bourbon, and would jump the fence and head for Tupelo.

Joe was right, a week later Squat was back in his straw mattress, stretched out and snoring soundly. The old dog died two days later, however. Dr. Little said he had no Idea what killed the old Pet. Might have been too much Bourbon, too much Red Tick, old age, or too much travel between Tupelo and Big Flat.

We had a family funeral in the back yard for squat. We would all miss the old dog for he seemed like a part of our family. Charlie said a prayer thanking the Lord for sending the hound our way. Pappy had a marker made thar read:

> ### Here lies squat: He is now at rest
> ### As hound Dogs go, Squat was the best.

Pappy would miss the old dog most of all. He had been his constant companion since we moved to Tupelo. I wandered if he would ever want another dog.

CHARLIE CALLOWAY

36

We Purchase The Lumber Company

IT TOOK ME TWO days to arrange a meeting with the current owners of the Highway 6 Lumber, and supply company. They were very open to hear of a potential offer from local investors. We sat down in the board room of our law firm two days later. Present at the meeting was Henry Grace, President of the company, William Defoe, Treasurer, and the company's private attorney, Josh Henry. Present representing the local investors were AC Calloway, Bonnie Little, Joe Webb, and Myself. Justin T Webb presided over the meeting and outlined what we would require before an offer was made. The list was rather short. But included a complete inventory of the stores in Tupelo, Columbus, and West Point.

We also wanted to review tax records of the business for the past five years and other financial documents including profit and loss statements. We also asked them to extend the deadline for closing the business for two weeks, or until we could accomplish the financial review.

In the end, the current owners agreed to our requests, except for the extension. They would only agree to one week. At the meeting they provided us with a list of all employees and their salaries, including management. That was unexpected but really appreciated, and very helpful.

Pappy said the company had added 20 new employees since he and Bonnie had sold the business. That included three additional Management positions. Expenses hat increased drastically, while revenue had declined. Pappy suspected it was because of lack of sufficient inventory.

Bonnie and Momma began the review of the books the next day, and Jannie McCullough provided a detailed inventory of the Tupelo store. Pappy had been right; Inventory of lumber and crucial supplies were down from when they sold the business by nearly twenty-five percent.

Pappy and Joe Webb spent three days going over inventory in Columbus and West Point. There too the inventory was way down. The company was living off the inventory. That was sure sign the company was losing money.

When all was said and done, Bonnie said she felt the business was worth no more than five Million. Buildings and inventory. We made an initial offer of 4.5 million. That offer was rejected. They wanted 5.5 million. We again countered with a five million dollar offer and they accepted. I agreed to put up half the money for a fifty percent ownership, Pappy and Joe Webb each agreed to put up 250,000 each. And Bonnie and Doctor Little were willing to invest one million. That left a Million to be financed by the First Mechanics Bank and trust. Company. However, Justin T. Webb, decided that he wanted a part of the business and put up the one million. We closed the deal a week later. We brought out the old sign from when the business was called Purnell, and Calloway Lumber and supply company. Most of the employees agreed to stay with us until we could get a management team in place. Mr. Webb had formed us a corporation. With each owner holding stock according to the percent that they had invested. I was appointed President and CEO, without a salary, Bonnie was treasurer and Pappy, and Joe Webb were titled Vice President, all the board were to be paid no salary for the first two years of operation. If the venture turned out to be profitable, dividends on the stock would be paid quarterly.

Pappy agreed to be our General Manager, and Bonnie would assist him, and they would work until we got the company back on sound footings. Joe wanted no part of working at the Lumber yard, but he and Notch McCullough would take up slack on the farm in Pappy's absence. Two weeks later we were off and running. Building inventory of lumber and supplies cost a lot of money. I loaned the company another 600,000 Dollars on a five year note at ten per cent interest, in order to get the stores back up to par. Color televisions were in demand, and we purchased nearly a hundred thousand in the newest televisions and refrigerators, washing machines, and other appliances. It began to pay off immediately. Sales topped anything that the previous owners had done. We were, however, over staffed everywhere, and was going to have to lay off a dozen employees. We decided to offer incentives to higher paid employees to encourage them to find other employment. Otherwise, they would have to take salary reductions.

The stockholders asked me to look into buying a Redi-mix concrete business that had come on the market in Tupelo. We took out a two hundred thousand loan with a local bank and purchased the *Bulldog Redi Mix* business from the owner who was ready to retire. The owner agreed to stay on and manage the operation for a year and train people to help run the operation. We relocated the business to the grounds of the lumber company. It was not a large operation. Three concrete mixer trucks and a mixing plant. It proved to be a good investment. All the management agreed to a ten percent reduction and move to the regular hourly wage crew. One employee agreed to move to West Point where we had an opening for an appliance salesperson.

While we were rebuilding the business, the War in Southeast Asia was heating up and Willy was called to active duty. We were worried about him, of course, for he would be flying B52 bombers into Viet Nam. When he got news that he was being called up to active duty, he asked the family to meet at Momma and Pappy's place for supper so that he could discuss his plans with us all. He brought Jessie along, and after dinner he announced that he had asked her to marry him and they would be married before he left for his assignment in 10 days. His stateside assignment was at Barksdale Air Force Base in Shreveport where he would train as co-pilot."

"Wow I said, that is quick. But we congratulated the two and asked where they were tying the knot."

"Here, he said, if it's all right with Momma and Pappy. We have little time for a big wedding or a honeymoon. That will have to wait. We will be leaving for Barksdale Air Force Base right after the wedding. They will have base housing ready for us. I will be in training both at Barksdale and Little Rock AFB for at least a month, and then I have no idea where I might be sent. We will honeymoon on the way to our assignment, I suppose. Jessie didn't seem overjoyed about that, but smiled as if she were all in.

I had not talked to Willy about Charlie and me, so I took the opportunity to tell him that we were also making plans for a wedding in late summer.

Willy looked stunned. You and Charlie are getting married?"

"Yeah, if she doesn't back out. We are going to build a house on the property the Pappy gave us. Hope to have it finished before winter."

"That's great he said, glancing at Pappy to see if there was any reaction. Why don't we make it a double? he asked.

I looked at Charlie for her reaction, she had a poker face.

"No, Willy, but thanks for asking. We are not quite ready just yet, I answered, but it was not that I wasn't ready, it was just that I didn't believe in double weddings. I did not want Charlie to have to share the spotlight with another woman. I had heard Momma say that the two of the most important days in a woman's life, was her wedding day and the birth of her first child. I didn't want a big wedding, but I wanted Charlie to be the center of attraction on her special day. I would explain that to Willy later, when we were to ourselves. I knew that Willy was excited about being called to active duty. Flying was what he had always wanted to do, and he loved military Life. I wasn't so sure about Jessie, however. How she would handle long periods of time without Willy around, I couldn't imagine. Oh well, that was none of my business. They set the date for one week from this day, and Momma, Charlie and Jessie went off to the kitchen to make plans. Pappy, Willy and me and Robert Lewis talking about his future in the Military. Willy had earned his Captain's bars and would likely be in training under a senior pilot, but he didn't seem to mind being second banana."

I too was a little concerned about my own military obligation. Although I was assigned to a guard unit, that was no real assurance that I would not be called to active duty either with my unit or without.

*"WILLOW YOU KNOW I'M A SOLDIER AND DUTY
ARE CALLING ME ON BUT IF I SHOULD FALL IN THE
BATTLE, DON'T SPENT YOUR LIFE LIVING ALONE."*

From the song "Willow" By Robert Coleman

37

Duty Calls Willy

A WEEK LATER WILLIE and Jessica were married in the living room of our home. I was his best man and Penny was maid of honor. ZJ was ring bearer, which he carried off perfectly, and Jessica's Dad gave the bride away. Mom had ordered a wedding cake for the occasion and she and Charlie and Jessica's mom served the refreshments. Willy's Commanding officer at the guard unit came with his wife and brought gifts. Joe Webb and Jannie McCullough came too, along with Naught. The house was crowded, but there was lots of laughs and speeches. The service was conducted by the Reverend Roy Cobb, the pastor of Mount NEBO Methodist church. The church where Jessica and her family had attended most of her life. The bride and groom left for Shreveport as soon as refreshments were served. I doubted if they would make it any further than West Point before stopping for the night, which was about an hour away. I wished that I had spent more time with Willy, for his mission would be a dangerous one and I loved my brother. He had always been there for me when we were growing up and every important decision that I made, I always ran it by Willy. Like Pappy, he always had a good insight on what was the right thing to do. He was not timid about telling me when he thought I was making bad choices. I had some doubts about his choice for a wife, but I said nothing to him, although I did discuss it with Charlie. Jessie was beautiful, smart and she exuded sexuality. I hoped my intuition about her were wrong for I didn't want to see Willy hurt. I think Pappy was having the same feelings about the girl, but he too kept mum about her.

"After the wedding we helped the newlyweds load their gifts into the back of Willy's truck along with some essentials for housekeeping'. We covered it all with a canvas tarp and tied it down securely. There were more hugs and kisses, until they finally pulled out of the driveway and waved goodbye. Momma was wiping tears away all the while.

It was getting late so ZJ said goodnight to the rest of the family, and we drove home. Charlie rode along with us. We needed a little time of our own. Once ZJ was tucked in, we sat in the porch swing and talked for an hour. We looked at the house plans that builders were to start construction on the next day. It was a Victorian style with a wrap-around porch. Another crew would start construction on the barn a hundred yards east of the house. She lay her head on my shoulder and kissed me tenderly, it was a special time for us. I asked her to stay the night, but she refused, and left me sitting in the swing, watching until she was out of sight. Five minutes later she called to tell me she was home and safe.

I had not heard from Gene Edwards since we had met in my office a week before, so I was surprised when he called.

"Just wanted to let you know, he said, that the Bureau has set a time and place for the funeral and burial of Lucas Robbins. The funeral will be at Mt. Zion church, about ten miles south of Lafayette Louisiana one week from today at 10:30. Burial will be immediately following the service. The body was badly mutilated, so there will be no public viewing of the remains. The Bureau is advising that the Calloway family, especially Charlie. not attend, but that will be up to you and your family. This is simply a precaution, so use your own judgment. It seems that after Lucas learned to write, he kept a diary, of such, and the only member of the family he talked in detail about, was Charlie. The Bureau recovered the diary from the two assassins, but they don't know if anything from the diary was passed on to someone else. I will be at the funeral if there is a family from Mississippi attending the service. Angela will accompany me."

I thanked the detective for the information and told him I would let him know what we decided. I was sure however, that the whole family would want to attend the funeral for they had become attached to the gentle blacksmith and felt it was a family obligation. At noon I went to a local gun shop and purchased a handgun. As an officer of the court, it was recommended that I carry a weapon. I chose a 32 caliber, nine-shot automatic. I also purchased an extra clip and fifty rounds of ammunition. If any of my family were to be in danger, I wanted us to be able to defend ourselves. I had only fired a pistol a few times in my lifetime and would need to go out to the farm and practice. I wanted Charlie to learn to shoot as well.

I put the proposition before the family that night at dinner. They all agreed that we should go to the funeral. We also included Joe Webb and Jannie. There was no way we could all travel in one vehicle to Lafayette. Pappy and Joe decided they would contract the trip out to a tourist agency and get a small luxury bus so that we could travel in comfort. I made reservations at the Holiday Inn in Lafayette for the whole Troop. We would spend the night before the service and the night after, before returning to Tupelo.

We left for Lafayette on August 1st. The trip took ten hours, but it was nice traveling together in a comfortable bus. The travel agency furnished a driver. Pappy was picking up the tab, so I figured he would fuss about the cost for a while. Momma was enjoying the trip however, so he wouldn't complain too much. Robert Lewis was staying with Bonnie and Doctor Little. The Doctor and Bonnie were taking him to see the Harlem Globetrotters play basketball in Memphis. He had been looking forward to the day for weeks. Bonnie was in charge of the lumber yard while we were away. We would check in with her from time to time to see if there were any problems.

We arrived in Lafayette at 4:30 in the afternoon and checked in to our rooms.

We decided to take dinner at Prejean's Cajun Restaurant where they had live Cajun Music, and a small dance floor. It surprised me when Momma and Pappy hit the dance floor. Joe and Jannie followed, and after some cajoling, I tried it with Charlie. It seemed that everyone had a terrific time, and I was glad because tomorrow would be a sad day when they laid Lucas Robbins to rest. We were back at the hotel before eleven with everyone exhausted from the long day. I wanted to be alone with Charlie but that would not happen tonight.

The next day we all gathered in the hotel restaurant for breakfast before leaving for the funeral. The Zion church was off the main highway about a mile in a wooded area. We pulled into the parking area of the small church just before ten. Gene Edwards and Angela were already there waiting in a patrol car. I asked the driver to pull in beside them. The pastor of the little church, James Broussard, encouraged his congregation to come to the funeral and about fifteen showed up. The church also furnished pall bearers to carry the casket. The pastor who was in his eighties had known The Robbins family when the boys were young and he shared a few kind memories, we learned that at least part of what Lucas had told us was true. Pastor Broussard said the boys never attended school. The burial took place in a little cemetery a hundred yards to the rear of the church. At the gravesite the pastor read a few verses of scripture from Romans XII, said a prayer, and the service was over. Lucas had been laid to rest. Charlie wept throughout the entire ceremony.

I spoke briefly with the pastor, thanking him for the kind words and his help with the funeral. I also spoke to Gene Edwards and Angela. Telling them we would be staying in Lafayette that night. The two detectives pulled out onto the highway, and we followed. There was a black Chevrolet Suburban right behind us. I assumed they were FBI. We were a quarter mile from the church and had just turned onto highway 182 north when a one-ton dodge truck, with a gigantic front grill burst from the brush smashing into the small tourist bus at the driver's door, sending it careening to the left and into a four-foot drainage ditch. Two men jumped from the truck with automatic weapons. I yelled for everyone to get on the floor. There was no argument. There was a hail of bullets hitting the van. I pulled the 32 automatic pistol from the belt holster at my back. I crawled to the front door and tried to push it open, but it was jammed into the side of the ditch. The driver had been hit and was slumped against the steering wheel, I pulled him into the floor, and he groaned so I knew at least he was alive. Gene Edwards and Angela had seen what was happening and did a U-turn and headed our way. There was an emergency exit mid-way on the right side of the bus. I crawled to it and kicked the latch open. Charlie had been hit I could tell but she was trying to crawl toward me. I motioned for her to stay down, and slithered out the door, and using the bank as a shield, I started returning fire. The men were back in the truck but there was no way to go except the way the truck came from. Edwards had the road blocked going north and the FBI had it blocked going South. I fired two shots at the side window and the driver slumped over the wheel; the truck lurched forward into the deep ditch. The other man had had enough. Jumped from the truck and raised his hands and Edward called and ordered him to get on his knees. He did as he was told.

I immediately went to the bus to check on the family and the driver. Charlie had been hit in the side and was losing a lot of blood. The driver had been hit in the right thigh and in the side just above the rib cage. His wounds were serious. With the help of the riders in the bus and the four FBI men and Edwards, we were able to push the bus out of the ditch. They didn't appear to be any mechanical damage to the bus. I got behind the wheel and headed north toward Lafayette with the two injured. Edwards led the way with lights and siren blaring. The FBI took charge of the two men in the truck. I did not know whether the driver of the truck was dead or not, but I was sure I had hit him. My concern was Charlie and getting her and the driver medical attention.

We were at the Lafayette Hospital emergency entrance in ten minutes. Edwards had called ahead on his radio and medical personnel were waiting with gurneys when I pulled the bus to a stop under the portico of the emergency entrance. Medical personnel loaded Charlie and the Driver, Mac Davis, onto gurneys and wheeled them away before I could get the bus parked. Momma and Pappy, Joe and Jannie were inside in the waiting area when I came in. Gene and Angela had been talking on the radio to the FBI agents and came into the room right after me. We learned that the driver had been hit in the neck and was unconscious. They would be at the hospital with their wounded prisoner in a few minutes. Momma had blood all over the front of her dress, where she had been attending to Charlie. No-one else was injured but everyone was pretty well shaken. It seemed like forever before the doctor came out and gave us a report.

"The young lady was seriously injured, and we had to perform surgery to remove two bullets from her right side. She has lost a lot of blood and it's going to be a while before we can tell you much more. There may have to be more surgery, but we have done all we can do for now. The driver of the bus, I am sorry to say, did not make it through the surgery; He died on the operating table. The young woman is in the ICU for tonight and we will reevaluate her condition in the morning. Meanwhile she is in very good hands," he said.

Gene Edwards told me that he would notify the bus company about the driver. "They will probably want to send another driver from Tupelo, and another bus, I'm sure the FBI will want to take charge of the bus. The driver of the truck was hit in the neck, but I think he will live, although he may wish he had not before it's all over."

The hospital and doctors allowed one person to stay in the ICU with Charlie overnight. Momma was wanting to stay but I told her firmly that I was going to stay. There was only a leather padded recliner in the room. Not a comfortable way to sleep, but I didn't figure to sleep much anyway. Momma, Pappy, Joe Webb and Jannie stayed until visiting hours were over and left for the hotel at eight o'clock. Charlie had been given enough pain medication that she was seeping soundly, but through the night she was very restless and cried out several times, calling my name. I went to her to try and comfort her, but she didn't seem to know that I was there.

A little after ten o'clock two doctors and a nurse came in and examined Charlie. They had no good news. The said that Charlie had slipped into a coma and all they could do was wait and see if her condition improved.

They advised me to let her rest for a while and then talk to her about things she is familiar.

"She apparently received a concussion in addition to the bullet wounds, there is a large bruise on her head and neck." The nurse will stay with her throughout the night and will call you if there is any change in her condition. There is just not much else we can do for her. Pray that she comes out of the coma quickly; we will do a brain scan and other e-ray's the first thing in the morning. Meanwhile, talk to her, it might help."

I called the hotel to tell Pappy what the doctor had said. He was very distraught but said he would tell the rest of the group.

I tried to sleep but sleep would not come. The nurse brought me coffee and a sandwich about ten and I ate and then settled back for a long, restless and worried night. I felt some guilt too for not telling the family in the beginning that we should not go to the funeral and stated it firmly. Charlie would have been angry, but she would not be in a coma now. Anger would have passed; I wasn't so sure about the condition she was in now.

38

Charlie's Condition Worsens

THE NEXT MORNING THE family was at the hospital before seven. We had a decision to make. I knew that the rest of the group needed to be back in Tupelo. The transportation company had sent a new bus and driver to return the group to Tupelo, I had called and talked with Mr. Webb and filled him in on the events of the last two days and told him that they would have to cover for me until Charlie could make the trip back home. Justin told me to take all the time I needed. I had no trial time scheduled which made it much easier for the firm to cover for me. Momma insisted that she stay with me, in Lafayette, and would not take no for an answer. She made arrangements for us to stay at the hotel for three more days. She would relieve me from time to time until the doctors said she could travel.

Hospital personnel took Charlie to Radiology for tests, and I waited outside the department in a small waiting area until they returned to her room. There seemed to be no improvement in her condition. Two hours later the doctor came in and asked me to follow him to his office where we could talk.

We took the elevator down to the first floor to the office of Doctor Richard Kirk. He took a seat behind a mahogany desk and offered me a chair immediately beside him. He rolled his chair around so he could face me. He leaned forward and spoke softly.

"Charlie is in bad shape; the bullet in her side did far more damage than we knew until we saw the scans. The bullet is lodged against her ascending aorta, the main artery from the heart. She is extremely lucky to still be alive. The bullet must be removed and will require surgery. I suggest that the surgery be performed right away. If the aorta is ruptured, there would be no way to save her. We have a fine surgeon here who can perform the operation, but it will require permission from parent or guardian. She is still in a coma, but I would advise the surgery to be done as quickly as possible. There was also damage, to surrounding tissue, and she also suffered a broken rib. Her recovery time is going to be extensive, I'm afraid," he added.

"When you say extensive, what do you mean, I asked?"

"Weeks, months, maybe more. Of course, that is only a guess. The coma is a serious concern, and we just have to hope it is only temporary. The brain scan showed no serious damage, only bruising and some swelling, but the scan doesn't show everything.

"I will call Charlie's Guardians now and they will come down and sign the necessary papers for you to conduct the surgery. Do you have any Idea, after the surgery, how long before we might move her to the hospital in Tupelo?" I asked.

"Not at this point. We do have a helicopter pad and a helicopter available. It would be rather expensive; but that would be the best way for her comfort. If that is what you wish to do, we will make the arrangements here and with the hospital in Mississippi."

I called Pappy at the hotel and asked them to come down quickly. Momma was a nervous wreck, and so was I, but I knew I had to be calm. I also had to decide what I was going to do about ZJ. I had told him that Charlie was hurt and was in the hospital. I told him that he might have to stay with Bonnie and Doctor Little for a few more days. He was alright with that, but I did not like being separated from him. I needed to convince Momma that she needed to get back home to see after ZJ.

Pappy and Momma were at the hospital minutes after my call and signed the necessary paperwork for the doctors to do surgery. An hour later they took her from ICU to the operating room. The three of us, Momma, Pappy and I waited outside in a family waiting area.

Two Louisiana State Police came by and asked a few questions but said that they had already talked with the Feds and didn't seem all that interested in what we had to say. We answered their questions and then they left. The doctors did not come out until an hour later.

I sat with Momma and Pappy and encourage Momma to return with Pappy to Tupelo saying that ZJ would need her in my stead. I told her I was going to have Charlie moved to Mississippi as soon as the doctors said it was safe for her to travel. I was going to have the hospital arrange the use of their helicopter to transport her. Momma finally agreed it was the best under the circumstances. In Tupelo we could arrange to have someone stay with Charlie around the clock. In Lafayette it would be nearly impossible.

Pappy called the bus company and told them they would not be returning on their bus, but they would be paid as agreed. They were staying one more night and would lease a rental car to make the trip back home.

When the doctors came out to talk, they said that the bullet had been remove, but she was still in a coma. Her vital signs were normal, which I took as good news. Momma and Pappy left me to return to the hotel and make arrangements for a rental car. They were on the road to Mississippi the next morning at six. I was alone with Charlie. I called and booked my room at the hotel for three more days, hoping the doctors would allow Charlie to be moved to The Hospital on the hill in Tupelo. However, two days later, she was still unresponsive and had developed a high fever. The Doctors said she had infection in her internal organs, and they were putting her on antibiotics to try and deal with the infection. It did not work, and Charlie's condition worsened; her breathing became labored. I felt helpless. The prognosis from the medical staff was not encouraging. I prayed.

Just after midnight, on the fourth day, the nurse came in and woke me. I was asleep with my head on the bed beside Charlie and I was holding her hand.

"There is a man outside in the waiting room. He says he is a friend and wants to see Charlie. He says his name is Luke.

"Luke? I don't think I know a Luke."

"Said he knew Charlie from Mississippi, that she taught him to read," she added.

"Lucas! What in the world, I thought? Let him come in,

"It's against the rules, but I'm going to allow him ten minutes."

Sue opened the door, and it was Lucas in the flesh. The funeral had been a ruse, and we all fell for it.

"I guess you are surprised to see me, and you must tell no one I was here. I am scheduled to testify on Thursday in New Orleans. I had heard the Feds, that were guarding me, talking about Charlie and that she was fighting for her life. And had a bad infection. They didn't think that she would live."

Lucas handed me two pills and told me to give them to her when he was gone, might stop the infection, he said, a gift from an old woman in the swamp. I don't know if they work or not. He reached over and took Charlie's hand, bent over and kissed her on the forehead, turned and walked out the door. When Lucas kissed her on the head her eyes seemed to flutter a bit and I thought she licked her lips as if she wanted water. I took a glass from the bedside table and poured about an ounce of water in the glass. I held Charlie's mouth open enough to place the two tiny pills on her tongue and gave her a sip of water. She swallowed. That was progress, I thought, but in seconds she was still. She remained that way until morning. I told no one what I had done. I just wanted Charlie to return to me and I was grasping at straws. She and ZJ were my whole life now and my whole future rested on my love for them, All I could do, however was to pray that he would not take Charlie from me.

"SOMEDAY WHEN WE MEET UP YONDER, WE'LL WALK HAND AND HAND AGAIN, IN A LAND THAT KNOWS NO PARTING. BLUE EYES CRYING IN THE RAIN"

Fred Rose

39

Charlie is Transferred

THE DOCTORS MADE THEIR rounds at seven in the morning. I had not slept since Lucas came by. I was tired and needed rest, but I was afraid to leave Charlie.

Dr. Barnes one of the two doctors, examined Charlie, wrote a few notes on her chart and said there was not much change, but the fever has subsided somewhat so the antibiotics may be working on the infection. I wondered though if it was the antibiotics or the pills that Lucas had given me. I probably would never know. Whatever was the case, Charlie was still in a coma. He suggested that I go and try to get some sleep, that the nurse would call me if there were any change in her condition.

I decided that he was right. I kissed Charlie on the lips and went to the hotel, showered and collapsed into the bed. I slept for eight hours. When I awoke, I dressed, called home and checked on ZJ and then the office to fill Justin in on what was happening. I then drove to the hospital. Charlie's condition had changed very little. The nurse told me that she was still running a high fever but was down a little since they had started a different medication. They were giving her nourishment intravenously. I pulled my chair beside her bed and talked to her about what was going on at home. That the construction crew were making good progress on our house and the barn crew was just about finished. I talked to her about wading in the creek and any good memory that came to my mind. Still there was no response.

On the fifth day after surgery, the doctors said they thought Charlie could make the three-hour helicopter trip to Mississippi. The chopper would be available the next day, so I called Pappy to tell him the approximate time of our arrival. We left Lafayette the next morning at eight thirty. There was an EMT the pilot, me and Charlie aboard. The chopper was new and was much quieter than I expected. The pilot had just returned from Vietnam where he chauffeured wounded soldiers from the battlefield to medical facilities near Saigon. He set the helicopter down at the North Mississippi Medical Center at 11;35, where we were met with other medical persons who carried Charlie on a gurney inside. I followed them to ICU where my parents were waiting just outside. I hugged them both while nurses got Charlie settled in the Intensive Care Unit.

Doctor Little waited with my parents. There would be more scans today he said and would give us a report the next morning. It was a Saturday so the Lumber yard would be closed at noon. Mrs. McCullough came shortly after noon with Notch to see about Charlie. The hospital was allowing no visitors until Charlie could be evaluated. Notch had been working at the lumber yard managing inventory while taking business course at the University Extension Service, He and his girlfriend were planning to be married in December. Notch had turned out to be a top-notch employee for the company, and had his eye set on management.

I learned from Mrs. McCullough that Naught had been wounded in a firefight in Vietnam, but his wounds were not life-threatening and would be awarded the Silver Star for his bravery, unfortunately he would be given a medical discharge and would be home as soon his doctors released him from a hospital in Germany. Mrs. McCullough was upset, of course, but relieved that he would be home soon.

I wondered what he would do once he was no longer a marine. The Marines had been his life for the past nine years. How would he adjust to civilian life?

Mrs. McCullough also announced that she and Joe were getting married in a week. They would not wait for Notch to return from the Marines. They would be married at Mount Nebo Baptist Church, with just a few close friends invited. She would take a week off from her job at the lumber yard. "We have not decided where we will go on our honeymoon, but it won't be far from home, she said, smiling.

I hugged her and told her I wished them both the best. "Joe is a fine man, and a good friend; I know you have made him very happy."

"My life will certainly be different," she laughed.

Shortly after Jannie left a nurse came out and told me I could go in and be with Charlie. Her condition had not seemed to have changed. She lay on the hospital bed with her long red hair spread out on her pillow. She was a beautiful woman, and my heart ached for her. I wanted to hold her and comfort her. I could do nothing, however, but wait.

Momma came by to stay with Charlie overnight so I could spend some time with ZJ, and perhaps get some badly needed sleep. I also needed to go to the office and get caught up on our pending cases. We were going to have to take turns staying with Charlie until she was out of the coma. I had to work at the law firm, they were swamped with cases and trying to cover for me. It was a difficult time, and I would have to do the best I could. I was surprised when I got a telephone call from Penelope. She said she had heard of Charlie's condition and was wondering if there was anything she could do to help. She said that she and Charlie had become close, and she would be happy to sit with her some.

"I get out of school about three thirty and usually home by four. I could sit with her for several hours each day if it would help."

"It would be a huge help, I said, thank you for calling. I am really grateful. We are stretched pretty thin right now."

"Just call me when you want me to come, she said, and I will be there."

"I will, and, again, thanks! I will call tomorrow", I said.

With Momma Pappy and Penny staying with Charlie during visitor hours, I was able to spend time at the law firm and be with ZJ at night. We had hired extra help at the lumber yard and Bonnie and Momma were training her to take Momma's place."

All of our plans were Moot, because Charlie's conditioned worsened each day and a week after we had moved her from Louisiana, Charlie died with me at her bedside holding her hand. So young, so beautiful; why did this have to happen. My heart was broken again. All the women I had ever loved were gone. What had I done to anger God so? In my heart I was asking God why he didn't just take me instead of the people I loved. I cried as I never had before. Momma and Pappy and Robert Lewis were devastated. It would take years before Momma would be able to talk about Charlie without crying. Pappy did not cry, but inside I knew how he was hurting. Robert Lewis was shattered and went off to himself for hours at a time. I could not console him nor could my mother. Robert had not just lost his sister, but Charlie was the rock that anchored him, his shelter from the storms they both had faced. She was in some ways my anchor too. She usually had a natural instinct for what was right and wrong, and she always spoke what she believed. Her funeral was held at the Church where we went many times when we were troubled, but I don't know if she was ever inside. The church was packed with fellow students and friends and family. I asked the preacher who had spoken at Annabelle's funeral to speak for Charlie. We buried her body on the hill above Big Flat where many of my relatives were buried. The funeral home had set up a canvas shelter for the family, and we listened as the Preacher read a few familiar verses from the book of Psalm, he prayed, and the ritual was over, no scriptures could ease the pain in my heart.

Pappy and Momma drove to the funeral in Pappy's truck for he wanted to talk to his cousin about getting a hound puppy. Squat had sired ten Pups and he wanted one that looked like his old friend. I was alone with ZJ, in the back seat of the funeral home furnished limo, I could not even explain my sorrow to my own son. He could sense my sorrow and laid his head in my lap and patted my leg. I kissed his head and spoke softly that I would be ok. I knew it would be a long time before I would be ok again.

When the funeral was over and the people and workers were gone, a lone man walked out of the woods, crossed the dirt road and knelt before Charlie's grave and placed a handful of flowers in front of her headstone. Lucas Robbins left the grave site, crossed back over the road and disappeared into the woods.

A week after the death of Charlie, Joe Webb and Jannie McCullough were married at Mount Nebo Baptist Church with only a dozen people present. I stood in the back of the church and marveled at how beautiful Mrs. McCullough looked. This was her day. Momma had arranged for a photographer to capture the entire event. Joe looked like Joe in his cowboy boots, jeans and a sports coat with a string tie. Pappy acted as best man and Momma was maid of honor. They all looked very happy.

Three weeks later, the city honored their Silver, and Bronze Star hero with a parade down Main Street with four marching bands, a unit of Marines and dozens of dignitaries from the city and state in their fancy cars. ZJ and I watched the grand parade from atop the Purnell and Calloway Lumber and Supply Company. Naught was a true hero and had overcome a lot of adversity to be a very proud Marine.

We moved into our house on the farm the week after the parade. It was the house that I dreamed Charlie and I would share for the rest of our lives. Now it seemed just a shell. ZJ was in school, and I sat alone on the big porch that looked out over this beautiful place, but what good was it without someone to share it with.

Thanksgiving had come and gone, and CJ was staying with Momma and Pappy over the holidays so he could play with a friend who had moved down the street near Momma and Pappy. I sat alone on the porch with a bottle of wine before me. It had become a ritual. After work I would have a drink or two to calm my nerves. I had just poured my second drink when Joe Webb came riding up on his big red mare. He dismounted and came upon the porch and sat in the other rocker. He was silent for a few seconds before he spoke.

"Does that stuff help? He asked."

"Helps me sleep sometimes."

"Speaking from someone who knows; You are not going to find the answer to your sorrow in that bottle. It will only make it worse for you and your son. Pour it out and get on with your life. He got up and mounted the red and rode away. I watched until he disappeared below the ridge.

He was right of course, and I did as he said. I had to think about my son. I took the empty bottles and threw them in the trash and vowed to myself not to take another drink. I switched to Iced tea in the afternoons and sometimes ZJ would have a glass with me. I had put up a basketball goal and backboard on the side of the barn and some afternoons we would shoot hoops after he finished homework. Other evenings we would just play catch with the baseball and a glove. On Saturday afternoons we would saddle the horses and ride over the farm. This was his favorite day of the week. Sometimes we would ride over to Joe and Jannie Webb's place. Jannie had really become attached and Joe as well.

This Saturday we rode along the ridge along a fence row where honeysuckle and wild roses grew, until we could see Joe's house in the distance. ZJ suddenly pulled his horse to a stop and slid down out of the saddle.

"What's wrong," I asked.

"Nothing, I have just got to piss, my nuts are floating," he said without changing expressions.

"Where did you learn such talk," I asked. I was dumbfounded.

"That's what Pappy says when he has to pee."

"I might have known. Guess I'll have to talk to Pappy about such talk. You just need to say, "I need to Pee."

"Ok," he said as he remounted the mare.

. As we drew closer to the Webb's, we could see the newlyweds on the porch painting an antique bedroom suite. They waved as soon as they saw us. We dismounted and walked up where they were working. Jannie offered us something to drink, but I said no, we didn't want to interrupt their painting. ZJ asked if he could help, and Joe said. "Sure, let's go get you a brush, and the two of them went off toward the shed. When they returned, I told ZJ we needed to go so Joe and Jannie could finish their work,

"Why don't you let him stay the night, so he can help Joe paint?" Jannie asked.

"Can I Dad?" ZJ begged.

"Well, we didn't bring any sleeping clothes."

"I'll take care of that, Jannie said, smiling. You can come for him first thing in the morning, and you can have breakfast with us."

"I promise I'll be good," ZJ said.

"Ok," I said, mounting up and taking the reins of ZJ's horse and leading him back across the ridge to our house. I unsaddled the horses, wiped them down and turned them in the lot behind the barn. I poured a bucket of oats and a bucket of corn in the trough. I went in the house showered, put on clean jeans and a Tee, poured myself a glass of sweet tea and went to the rocker on the front porch to listen to the crickets and the crickets

I turned the radio on and was listening to the Grand Ole Opry out of Nashville. I was already missing ZJ, even though I knew he was with good friends who loved him and would take good care of him. I realized that I needed my son as much as he needed me. It crossed my mind to get in the truck and go after him, but I knew that would not be fair to him or to the Webb's.

The sun was just beginning to set behind the tall pines along the highway casting long shadows across the meadow, when I saw headlights turn off the highway and onto the gravel road that led up to my house. I watched until it came up the ridge and into my yard; there was no mistaking the red '57 chevy convertible.

*"YOU KNOW THAT I LOVE YOU AND I ALWAYS
WILL, BUT THERE'S AN EMPTINESS INSIDE
ME NOW THAT NOTHING SEEMS TO FILL."*

"Y0u Know That I Love You"/Robert Coleman

40

A Surprise Visitor

IT WAS PENELOPE JOHNSON. When she pulled into the yard, I came down off the porch to greet her. She had the top of her convertible up, so I spoke to her through the driver's side window. "What a nice surprise. Are you lost?" I asked.

"No, it was probably a mistake, but I just thought I would stop by and see how you were doing; I wasn't sure you would even speak to me after the things I said to you the last time we talked. If you don't want to talk to me, I will understand and will leave."

"No, you had every right to say what you did, for it was all true. But I am not, nor have I ever been a womanizer. I hope you believe that. It's good to see you. I'm glad you came. Can I offer you a glass of Iced tea?"

"Sure, she said. And I would like a tour of your new house if you don't mind. It is beautiful from the highway"

"Sure," I led the way up the steps, and went to the refrigerator, took Ice cubes from the trays and filled her glass and then poured her a glass of sweet tea. "Follow me, I nodded with my chin, and I'll give you the grand tour. I have to warn you, I'm not the world's best and neatest housekeeper. I've been trying to find a housekeeper, but no luck so far. I guess I'm just too choosy."

I led the way up the stairs where there was two bedrooms and a bath and a space for an office that I never used. "Momma and Jannie Webb decorated and bought the furnishings, at my expense of course, but I was pleased with what they did.

I led the way back down the stairs to the master bedroom and ZJ's room

"The house is beautiful, but not ostentatious, she said smiling."

"Ostentatious. Big word. Is that the kind of person you think I am?"

"Well, it crossed my mind at one time, but I'm really glad I was wrong. It is just perfect; I love it."

"We have two bedrooms downstairs, I added, the master bedroom and ZJ's room. However, we are bunking together at the present time. I haven't had the heart to make him sleep in his own room. Losing his mother has been very hard for him, and then we lost Beverly, the housekeeper. That was difficult for him too, but he seems to be adjusting slowly.

"I wouldn't worry about it, Penny said, he will probably decide on his own, soon enough, to go to his room. It wouldn't look good if his friends learned he was still sleeping with his parents.

"Yeah, I guess you're right."

"How is the teaching job going? I asked."

"Great. I love my Job and the kids. And you?"

"Good, but I am really stretched thin right now, since we bought the lumber company. We are trying to get a management team in place, but it's been a slow process. There just doesn't seem to be enough hours in the day to get everything done that I need to do."

"Yeah, I heard how you saved the lumber company from closing. That was a nice gesture. A lot of people are very grateful for what you did. You are a good man in my Pop's eyes, and mine," she added.

"Are you seeing anyone now?" I asked.

"Well. Let me think, she said, putting her index finger against her temple. I think I have had two dates in the past two years, one with a high school football coach. He was not interested in a relationship, just a one-night stand. I was back home by eight-thirty. The other was with a young preacher just out of the seminary. He was looking for a missionary wife to go with him to spread the gospel in Africa. He was a nice enough fellow, but that was not in the top one hundred things I wanted to do with my life. I never heard from him again. I guess grown men are just not attracted to me. The men in my life are seven years old and in the second grade; they seem to love me just fine, she laughed."

"I can imagine, I stammered, I never had a beautiful teacher like you when I was in school."

"I think you just gave me a compliment: thanks, I needed it."

"What is the worst part of your life right now?"

I asked, looking directly into her eyes, as if I were looking for some deep truth that she would be afraid to reveal.

She didn't answer right off; she gazed out into the darkness and then turned and looked at me with tears forming in her beautiful blue eyes. It was obvious that she was hurting inside and just needed to tell someone, and she seemed grateful that I asked.

"Loneliness," she finally said. "I love my job and I love Pop, but it's not enough. The rest of my life just seems empty and meaningless,"

"I looked at her intently, before I spoke. "I know what you are saying, I too have a great job, a great son, and more money than I will ever spend, but it just means nothing without someone you love to share it with. Like there is an emptiness inside me that just can't be filled."

We sat on the porch and talked until midnight. She called her father to tell him that she was going to be late. She gave him no indication about where she was, or what time she would be home.

While she was on the phone, I grabbed a blanket from the bedroom closet for the weather had turned much cooler. We pulled the rockers closer together so we could share the blanket.

"Thanks, she said, and I suggest we make a cup of Coco to warm us."

"Show me the kitchen and I'll make it", she said.

We made our coco in two large mugs and went back to the rockers. She talked about her father who was in failing health. He was no longer able to work in his auto repair shop and she was seriously worried about him. He could walk no more than a few steps without having to rest. She was at a loss, for he refused to seek medical help.

Finally, just before midnight, she said she had to go. "I have probably already overstayed my welcome."

"No, it's been fun just talking to you. I hope I haven't bent your ear too much; I know I have unloaded a lot on you."

"No, she said, quite the opposite. I feel better knowing that someone else has the same feelings that I have."

She got up to leave and I followed her to her car.

"I hope you will come back again, soon," I said.

"I will, but you will have to call me. I don't like just dropping in on someone without notice."

"I will call, for sure"

I had an urge to take her into my arms and hold her and ask her to stay, but I knew it was too soon for us both. We needed some time to let our emotions ebb.

She slid in behind the wheel, I shut the door, and said goodnight; she made a U-turn in the drive, and I was standing there alone, a pang of sadness tugged at my heart. I watched the taillights of her car until she turned onto the highway, off the gravel road, and disappeared into the darkness,

I went to my room, shed my jeans and crawled into bed. It was a long time before I slept, thinking of Penny Johnson and our conversation.

It had been barely three months since Charlie had passed and she was still in my heart, but Penny was, nevertheless, on my mind. Perhaps, the storms in my life were finally passing, and the sun was going to shine once more.

"A MAN THAT DOESN'T READ IS NO BETTER OFF THAN A MAN WHO CAN'T READ."

Mark Twain

41

Another Surprise Visitor

THE NEXT SATURDAY AFTERNOON, just after mid-day, ZJ and I were getting ready to saddle the horses for a ride over the farm when I heard the sound of a vehicle turn off the main road onto the drive that led up to our house. It sounded if it had no muffler. I watched until it came into view. It was a beat-up old Dodge flatbed truck with sideboards. "It couldn't be, I thought," but it was, LUCAS the blacksmith. I walked out to greet the old friend when he pulled to a stop and got out. ZJ was right behind me. Lucas looked the same as he did the last time I had seen him several months ago, except that now he had a full beard.

He slid out of the truck, and I offered my hand; he shook it firmly. I introduced him to my son. Lucas bent over and took the boy's hand and smiled. "Fine looking boy you have there, he said."

"Lucas, it's good to see you, but I must say, it is quite a surprise. I thought you were still with the Feds."

"Not anymore, the trial was over weeks ago, I gave my testimony, and those two old boys are in jail for life, and they turned evidence against a dozen or so others of their own kinds. I opted out of the program. I figured they had enough problems that they would not be concerned about me. I was wondering if my old shop on the farm is still available?"

"Well, that will be up to Pappy, but I'm sure he would love to see you back in business, on the farm. We took your sign down when you left, but Pappy has it in the barn, hoping that you would return some day. Come on in the house and I will call him. I'm sure he will want to see you."

"I wanted to tell you too, how sorry I am about what happened to Charlie. I loved that child."

"Yeah, I know, I loved her too, we all did. Sometimes there is just no explaining why the Lord allows things to happen to such good people."

ZJ and I led the way up the steps and Lucas followed but took a seat in one of the rockers on the porch.

"If you don't mind, I'm going to wait out here, it is a beautiful view over the farm from here. I have sure missed this place."

"Sure, I said, I'll be right back. Can I offer you something to drink?"

"No, I'm good he said. I've got another matter I need to ask you about if you have a minute."

"Ok, I said, I'll be right out."

I called the house, but Momma said that Pappy was on his way out to the farm.

"He left about ten minutes ago with his new Pup. His cousin brought him the dog from Big Flat yesterday. He calls him Smokey. He sticks to AC like glue.

I went back to the porch and told Lucas what Momma had said, I told him to follow me, and we would go to meet Pappy at the barn.

We made it to the barn just a minute before Pappy drove up. He got out of his truck with Smokey at his heels, ZJ clapped his hands when he saw the pup and the dog came right to him. ZJ ran down the road toward the pond with the pup right behind him all the way.

I could tell by the look on his face that Pappy was overjoyed to see Lucas again.

Pappy and Lucas shook hands, and both were grinning like a monkey with a banana.

"Lucas what in the world are you doing in these parts, I thought we buried you in Louisiana? Pappy laughed."

I had told Pappy about Lucas coming to the hospital to see Charlie, but I had told no one else.

"That was what the Feds wanted everyone to think, and the plan worked pretty good, but I asked to be released from the program after the trial was over. Was wondering if I might have my old blacksmith shop back and get back in business."

"Sure, Pappy replied. It's just like you left it. We'll have to put your sign back up, and run an ad in the Journal to let folks know you are back in business. Notch McCullough is living in the old Davis house now that Jannie Jo Webb are married. Notch says that he plans to be married soon. He will be a good neighbor. Your living quarters are the same as when you left. I'm going to see about adding on to your quarters and putting in running water and a bathroom. It's time you had a decent place to live."

"I see you have your tools on your truck, if you want to, just back it in the shop and we'll help you unload,' I offered.

An hour later we had his equipment unloaded. ZJ helped with the lighter tools and smokey followed him every step. Later Pappy and Lucas went down to the highway and put the sign in its original place. ZJ and I went to the journal and put in a small ad to run for a week, and then drove back to the farm.

NOTICE

"Lucas Robins, the blacksmith is back in business. Horseshoeing, welding, Plow sharpening, and harness repair. Open 6 to 6, Monday through Saturday noon. Call TUP5555 for information."

I will let Joe and Jannie know that he might be getting phone calls, and we will all spread the word." If you need anything else just let me know.

"Well, there is one thing, Lucas said. When I left, the County sheriff had a warrant for my arrest, and I need your help in getting that matter behind me. I don't know if he still wants to see me or not,"

"I doubt if the warrant is still outstanding, but I will look into it the first thing Monday morning. Meanwhile you can get your equipment put away and your living quarters squared away. Expect you will need *some food too.*"

"I've got enough in the truck to last me a few days, and the feds left me in pretty good shape as far as cash goes, but I will need to go into town Monday for supplies."

ZJ and I left Pappy and Lucas sitting on bales of hay talking, for my son and I were having dinner with Penny and her dad. She wanted to let her dad meet ZL. We would miss our Saturday afternoon ride over the farm, but ZL liked Penny and was ok with that. Penny and I had talked every day since she stopped by, and I gave her a tour of our house. She was the sunshine in my life now, and I could not wait to see her. I wanted to ask her to marry me, but I wanted her to talk to her dad about living with us on the farm. I hoped she would do it right away. We had plenty of room, and he could rent his house and shop for enough for him to have a nice income, and if his health improved, Lucas could always use help in the blacksmith shop.

Pop and ZJ hit it off right away and before we left, he was teaching ZJ how to play checkers. They were both rattling on about cars.

Life rarely unfolds as we imagine, and I have decided that is a not a bad thing, Penelope came to me at an unexpected time in my life and filled the emptiness in my heart.

SEVEN MONTHS LATER

Penelope Johnson and I were married on the steps of the First United Methodist Church on the first day of June 1965. Willy was home on leave from his first tour in Viet Nam. He was my best man and Jessie; his wife was maid of honor. Momma, Pappy and Robert Lewis, the entire Webb law firm was present along with many teachers from the school where Penny taught. Unnoticed by most of those present was Naught McCullough. He stood in the deep shadows of the giant Oak trees across the street from the old church. If someone had looked closely, they would have seen teardrops on his cheek, that ran down and dripped off the silver star that was pinned to his chest.

Annabelle Owens was my first true love, and I guess those memories and feelings never quite leave you, no matter how much you may love someone else. I love Penelope with all my heart, but sometimes in the silence of the midnight, Anna's smile comes to me, and I am awakened from my slumber, feeling that she is near, and sometimes when I visit the old church on Jefferson, I sometimes think I catch her scent on the Magnolia wind.{1}

{1} From a song by John Prine, "Magnolia Wind"

THE END

Epilogue

On June 1, 1994, Penelope Johnson and I celebrated our thirtieth wedding anniversary. Present were our four children, ZJ. 35, a partner in the Webb and associates Law firm. The triplets, Allie, Annie, and Arden, 28. They were there with their children and their Husbands. All three of our girls attended the "W," to my dismay, and earned degrees in Nursing and are working at the North Mississippi Medical Center and live within ten minutes of their parents, and usually show up at our house on Sunday afternoons for lunch.

Pappy died in May of last year of a cerebral Hemorrhage while mending a fence on the farm, and Momma a month later; we guess of broken heart. She just couldn't adjust to the loss of the love of her life. I miss them terribly. Pappy had made provisions in his will to leave each of his children and grandchildren fifty thousand dollars. That included Robert Lewis, which he considered his own, although he was never adopted. The balance of his cash estate he left to the City of Tupelo for the purpose of building a shelter for the homeless. It amounted to more than a half million dollars. The farm property that he and Momma owned he left to me and Willy equally. It amounted to two hundred acres each.

Momma and Pappy were buried in the old necropolis on the hill that overlooks Big Flat, where our relatives had been buried since the early 1800's.

Willy retired from the Air Force after thirty years as a pilot. He earned the rank of Lieutenant Colonel. After retirement he purchased a small passenger plane and has a charter business that makes regular flights to Birmingham, Jackson, and the Gulf coast of Alabama. He and his wife Jessie have two children, Janett Marie, and William Zachery. They Live a half mile away on the Land that Pappy deeded him when he graduated from Ole Miss. Their daughter 21, is a senior at Ole Miss and has been accepted to the University of Mississippi School of Medicine, and his son 22, is a freshman at the Air Force Academy.

Willy and I are still very close. He Taught me to fly and sometimes, if I have time, I fly with him, usually acting as his co-pilot. I wanted to buy a small Cessna single engine for the Law firm, but Penny said no; to leave the flying to Willy. That ended the discussion.

Justin Webb the founder of the Webb law firm passed away ten years ago at the age of ninety, leaving the firm and all the assets to me and his nephew Jackson Webb. Leaving me a majority stockholder. He came to the firm every day until a few days before his death, but he would only stay a few minutes as he took his daily walk around the city that he loved. He would never fail to stop at the courthouse, saying hello to his old friend, the circuit judge.

His nephew works for the firm full time now and has turned into a fine lawyer. I look forward to the day that ZJ will take over the firm, and Penny and I can travel this beautiful country. ZJ is thirty-five now and is a fine lawyer. He is also a member of the Mississippi State Senate. He spends about as much time helping to make laws as he does defending those that break them,

Joe Webb and Jannie still live in the same house they lived in when they were married. Joe is in his late seventy's still is in great shape, rides his horse every day. Jannie is still a beautiful woman in her seventies. They are some of our dearest friends and are regular visitors in our home.

Naught McCullough, who had received a Medical Discharge for wounds he sustained in Viet Nam reapplied for active duty in the Marines, and with the help of his congressman was assigned as a recruiter in West Point. He retired after twenty-seven years and lives in Tupelo. He never married.

Notch McCullough married his High School girlfriend, and they have five children. Notch is General Manager of the Purnell and Calloway Lumber and supply Company. He is a tireless worker and has earned an associate degree in business from the University Extension Service.

Doctor Little Passed away four years ago and Bonnie still lives in their house on the lake. She comes by the Lumber Company nearly every day and is still active in charity work in Tupelo.

The city has changed much since Pappy moved us here in 1951. The old drugstore is still in use but is not a popular hangout as when I had my first date with Anna. The old theater is still here and is still in use, but there is talk that it will be closing soon. The school where we attended and I met the beautiful Annabelle Owens, is still a school, but is now a Jr. High School. The old Presbyterian church has been added on to but is still has an active membership and is as beautiful as ever. I still go there from time to time when I am troubled about something and just want a quiet place to think. Change is inevitable in people and places, but all and all I think Annabelle would be pleased with what her town has become.

Robert Lewis is a professional baseball coach. After he graduated from Ole Miss, he was drafted by the St. Louis Cardinals, and played third base for six years. He is now a manager of their AAA farm club. Willy flew Penny and me on two occasions to watch him play. I am happy that Momma and Pappy lived long enough to watch him. He was an outstanding player until a shoulder injury ended his playing career.

Printed in the United States
by Baker & Taylor Publisher Services